PROPOSING TO THE CHILDREN'S DOCTOR

CHAPTER ONE

'THIS is all getting out of hand,' Rebecca murmured. 'That's another glass that's been smashed, and Susie already has a cut on her foot from the vase that was broken earlier.'

She knelt down to gingerly pick up the broken shards of a drinking glass, frowning as she watched a group of young men work their way through the crowded room, bumping into people and furniture as they stumbled on their way to the kitchen where the temporary bar had been set up.

She pushed the silky fall of her chestnut-coloured hair back over her shoulder so that she could concentrate better on what she was doing. Her head was throbbing, possibly something to do with the thundering sound of heavy rock music that reverberated through the ground-floor flat and made the floorboards judder in reaction.

Carefully, she dropped the jagged pieces of glass into a waste-paper basket and then stood up.

'Who are those people, anyway?' she asked, directing a troubled glance towards her friend, Angie. 'Did you invite them to the party?'

Angie gave a negligent shrug. 'Wasn't me. I expect they're medical students who heard about the party and decided to crash it. I wouldn't worry too much about them. I expect they'll sober up a bit once they get some food inside them.'

'Hmm. Maybe.' Rebecca's grey eyes were troubled, but Angie wasn't going to allow her to be concerned for long.

She angled the wine bottle she was holding out over Rebecca's glass. 'Have another drink, Becca…You need to chill out… This is your last night here and we mean to see you off in style.'

Rebecca gave a brief smile. Angie meant well, but the last thing Rebecca needed right now was to find herself in the middle of a surprise going-away party when she still had packing to do and last minute problems that had arisen which meant she had to go to work in the morning. As it was, all her travel plans had been thrown into disarray and she had to sort out alternative arrangements in order to transport her belongings to the old cottage up in Scotland.

What she wanted was peace and quiet so that she could wind down after her difficult day at the hospital and a clear head so that she could think for a while, and it didn't look as though either of those scenarios was going to be available to her any time soon.

'Perhaps we should turn the music down a little,' she suggested, 'before the neighbours start complaining. Did you invite any of them to join us?'

Angie made a face. 'I thought about it, but I wasn't sure they would be into the party scene. Next door are getting on a bit, and anyway they've been out all day, so I haven't had a chance to talk to them. I wanted to invite the new tenant from upstairs, but I haven't seen anything of him either, since he only moved in last night.' Angie rolled her eyes. 'Now, there's someone I'd really, really like to have around. He's definitely my kind of guy with those dark good looks and devil-may-care eyes that make me go hot all over, just thinking of him.'

Rebecca laughed. 'You don't even know the man. He could be a mass murderer for all you know.'

Angie grinned. 'I don't care. I'll take my chances.'

Rebecca made a wry face. She had reservations about the new tenant. Her first impression of him hadn't been all that great. He had arrived at the house after darkness had fallen yesterday evening, with nothing more than an overnight bag to his name, as far as she could tell. What kind of tenant had no proper luggage?

Struggling to wake up, she had come across him in the early hours of the morning as she'd left for work, putting his key into the lock of the main door of their building. At the time they had simply exchanged brief nods in greeting.

She had sent him nothing more than a hurried glance, but it had been enough for her to take in his rugged frame and the slightly crumpled appearance of his clothes, a linen shirt open at the neck and black trousers that clung to strong legs. There was a hint of dark shadow about his face, as though he had forgotten to shave.

She was used to people coming and going from the top-floor flat. The previous tenants had worked on short-term contracts and had rented the place for about six months before they'd moved on, and she guessed this man would be no different.

Not that she would be staying around to get to know

him. After all, this was the last full day she would be spending in the area, and after her one final obligation to the hospital was fulfilled tomorrow, her work there would come to an end.

A bang distracted her just then, followed by a muttered oath, and she turned to see one of the medical students, who had lurched against a bookcase, catching his ribs on the wooden corner of the unit, books tumbling to the floor. She pulled in a deep breath.

'Perhaps you should go and sit down over there,' she suggested, indicating a chair with the flick of her head. She tried to steady the young man with her hand while she struggled to prevent the bookcase from falling over with the other.

'I've got it,' Angie said, coming to help, and between them they managed to gently ease him down into a chair.

Rebecca looked back at the pile of books and stifled a sigh. Even the boisterous children on the paediatric recovery ward at the hospital didn't cause this much chaos.

Another sound stopped her in her tracks as she began to pick up the fallen items and replace them on the shelves. 'Did you hear that?' she asked Angie.

Angie shook her head. 'Can't hear anything above this din. I thought you turned the sound down a little while ago.'

'I did.' Someone had obviously decided that had been a bad move on her part, though, because now the noise was as loud as ever and she could barely hear herself think. Still, underneath it all she could just about make out a knocking sound. Rebecca frowned, trying to make out where the noise was coming from. 'Someone's at the door,' she murmured.

It was probably one of the neighbours, coming to complain, and she steeled herself to go and pacify whoever it was. She had always got along well with the people next door, but there was a limit to what they could be expected to cope with.

Pulling open the door to the flat, an apology was already forming on her lips, but it faded rapidly as she looked out to see the man from the top-floor flat standing in the hallway.

'Oh, it's you,' she said awkwardly. 'I thought it might be someone else.'

He shook his head. 'Did you? I've been banging to get your attention for a while, but I'm glad that it was you who opened the door. I was hoping that I would be able to catch up with you some time today.'

'Were you?' Puzzled, Rebecca pulled the door almost closed behind her in an effort to shut out some of the noise. She studied him guardedly. Why would he be trying to catch up with her? She didn't know him, or anything about him, except what she had managed to glean last night in the few moments when their paths had crossed. 'You're not here to complain about the noise, then? I've been trying to keep it down.'

'Have you?' His mouth made a wry twist. 'I suppose it all depends how you interpret keeping it down.'

She slowly absorbed the implied criticism and pushed it into the background. 'You know how it is… People get to drinking and then they want to dance, and before you know it they're tuned in to the beat and it all gets a bit crazy.'

'Yes. Anyway, that's not actually what I'm here about.'

'Oh…I see.' She frowned. Why on earth would he be seeking her out? He was a stranger to her. The only thing they had in common was that they both kept late hours.

Perhaps he read her thoughts because he said, 'I'm Craig, by the way. Craig Braemar.'

'I'm Rebecca.' She acknowledged the introduction with a faint inclination of her head. When all was said and done, she didn't want to appear unfriendly, even if he was there to complain about something else. It wasn't her way, no matter how distracted she might be. 'Of course, you could always join us, if you'd like to?' After all, it could be a better move to pull in the opposition rather than have him create problems for her.

'Thanks, it's tempting, but I actually need to grab some more sleep and I want to keep a clear head for the morning. I'm expecting a call.'

'That's OK. It was just a thought. I wouldn't like you to feel that we were leaving you out.'

She studied him surreptitiously. Maybe he'd been out on the town last night and was still recovering. Whatever the circumstances, he was definitely more presentable today than he had appeared to her then, and she had to admit to herself that his voice surprised her, too. There was a vibrant, deep quality to it, and it somehow managed to wrap itself around her senses in a most unexpected way.

Today he was clean-shaven, and the clothes he was wearing were considerably more respectable than those of the night before, a fresh dove-grey cotton shirt beneath a black leather jacket and black denims that followed the line of long, strong-looking legs. His hair was a crisp, midnight black, cut in a short, cropped style, and his jaw was square, as though he brooked no nonsense from anyone. His eyes were a subtle mix of blue and grey, and right now his gaze homed in on her, returning her stare with laser-like precision, making her shift uneasily.

His glance shimmered over her, taking in the feminine curves outlined by the soft fabric of the strapless dress that clung where it touched and ended in a swirl of silk that draped itself around her knees.

His gaze was dark and brooding. She had no idea what he was thinking and for some reason that she couldn't define, that bothered her. Was he dismissing her as a feckless airhead who went in for wild shindigs and a chaotic lifestyle?

Why should his impression of her rankle, anyway? He was nothing to her, and she didn't want to acknowledge that he had tweaked her interest in any way. She was off men. They were trouble, big time, and most likely he would prove to be no exception.

Even so, she kept up an appearance of civility. 'Is there a problem?' she asked. 'I know it can't be easy moving into a new place. If there's anything I can do to help, you only have to ask.'

'It's nothing like that, but thanks all the same.' His tone was faintly dismissive, and she stiffened, returning his look with a questioning, watchful expression.

'It's about a phone message that was left for you just after you went out this morning,' he said. 'It was obviously someone who doesn't know you too well, because she rang the number of the communal phone. It was only by chance that I heard it as I was crossing the lobby.'

Rebecca's eyes widened a fraction. Who would be calling her here? All her friends and family had her mobile number. Unless something had happened to—

'It was someone who lives near to your aunt, I believe,' he murmured. 'At least, she said she was a neighbour, Margaret, and she told me that your aunt was unwell. Nothing too serious, she thinks, but she's not quite herself, and she's been feeling a little dizzy lately. She said she would keep an eye on her over the next week or so, but she wondered if you might manage to get over there to see her some time soon.'

'Oh, I see.' Rebecca tried to absorb the information that confirmed her worst fears. Aunt Heather was ill? That was deeply distressing news, all the more so because her aunt had been like a mother to her. She had taken Rebecca and her sister under her wing and given them all the love and care that it had been possible for her to give through a good part of their young lives. It was unthinkable that she should be virtually alone in her island home while her family was so far away.

She glanced up at the man. 'Well, thank you for letting me know. That's a message I definitely needed to get.'

He nodded. 'That's what I thought. It's difficult when elderly relatives are left to fend for themselves.'

Was that a hint of censure she detected in his voice? Rebecca drew herself up, a spark of resentment flaring to life in her smoke-grey eyes. What did he know about the way she lived her life? Who was he to stand in judgement of her?

She opened her mouth to say something, but then clamped it shut as he went on, 'Actually, there was something else—I found a letter addressed to you this morning.'

He reached into his inside jacket pocket and drew out an envelope, holding it out to her. 'This is you, right— Rebecca McIntyre?'

Rebecca nodded, and he said shortly, 'I thought so. I heard your flatmate calling out after you, this morning as you left the house. I would have given it to her to pass on to you, but I was having a bit of a lie-in, and after that I was out for some of the day, so I haven't had the chance to catch up with either of you.'

Her glance flicked over him. Nice that he was able to grab a leisurely day for himself. She couldn't remember the last time she had been able to do that. Her job was one of constant pressure, with lifesaving decisions to be made about her small patients and long hours when she was on call.

Still, to be fair to him, maybe he was taking a day or so to acclimatise himself to his new surroundings. At any rate, it didn't sound as though he had anything pressing he needed to attend to right away, no job to keep him occupied.

He gave her a grimace. 'I don't know who picked up the letter originally, but it might be that it slipped from a pile on the hall table and somehow became wedged between the table and the wall. I caught a glimpse of the corner of the envelope. The postmark is a few days old, so I hope it wasn't anything important.'

He handed her the envelope and she stared down at the black, handwritten address and winced. The writing style was familiar enough. She would recognise her sister Alison's neat lettering anywhere, but why would she write and not phone? There was an overseas postmark, and that could only mean that there had been some kind of setback to her plans and she wasn't able to come back to the UK as planned.

She released a faint sigh. All her plans for a joyful reunion were falling apart. This day was getting worse with every moment that passed, and on top of that her new neighbour must be thinking that she was careless and irresponsible along with everything else.

'Thanks again,' she murmured, sending the man a quick glance. 'I do appreciate the trouble you've taken.'

'You're very welcome.' He frowned. 'Though I take it from your expression that it's not likely to be good news in there?'

She gave a reluctant smile. 'Don't worry. I won't shoot the messenger. All in all, it's been a bad day for me, but things can only get better, can't they?'

'Let's hope so.' He made as though to move away from her, but in that instant a crashing sound erupted from inside the flat, followed by a loud scream.

He turned around to face her once more, his expression rueful. 'I think perhaps you might have spoken too soon,' he murmured.

Rebecca felt her heart sink. 'Oh, dear. I'd better go and see what's going on in there. Thanks again for passing on the message.'

She turned away from him and pushed open the door to the flat, standing in the doorway and scanning the room briefly. It was clear at a glance what had happened.

The heavy, glass-fronted display cabinet had fallen over, probably aided by some drunken partygoer stumbling about, and she could see that some of the contents, once beautiful glassware and delicate ornaments, were scattered in fragments about the floor.

Far worse than that, though, a man's arm was sticking out from underneath the cabinet, and a pool of his blood was slowly seeping across the carpet. People were standing about, some in shock, some confused and most the worse for wear through drink.

'Help me get the cabinet off him,' she said in an urgent tone, rushing over to where the man lay and directing her words at her friends. 'Angie, can you grab one end? Connie, will you go around the other side?'

Angie's new flatmate hurried to position herself at a point where she could assist. 'It's too heavy,' Connie said. 'We're not going to be able to do this on our own.'

'You girls get ready to pull him out from underneath.' Craig's voice cut into their conversation, his tone clipped and decisive, and Rebecca stared up at him in shock. He must have followed her into the room. 'I'll ease it up from him. Just watch out for falling glass.'

'Perhaps we should find something that we can wedge in between him and the glass doors when you lift it?' Angie's expression was stricken. 'He's already badly cut, from the look of things. Wait just a second while I go and grab something from the kitchen.'

She hurried away and came back just a moment or two later, armed with a couple of large trays. 'I'll try to slide these over him as you move him out of the way.'

Rebecca nodded, and glanced at Connie. 'We need to keep his head and neck as steady as possible while we drag him out from underneath.' She looked around for more volunteers, and a trio of men came forward. One of them went to help with the cabinet.

'Are you ready?' Craig asked. 'Is everyone in position?'

'We're ready.' Rebecca signalled to the others, and in a team effort they pulled the young man clear of the cabinet while Craig and his helper stood it back on its feet.

'He's losing an awful lot of blood,' Angie said. 'There are cuts to his arm and wrist. He'll need to go to hospital.'

Rebecca nodded. 'There's a puncture wound to a main blood vessel. Ring for an ambulance while I try to stop the bleeding, will you?'

'I've already called emergency services,' Craig said. 'Do you have anything you can use as a pressure pad?'

'Yes, in the first-aid bag.' She was already applying pressure to the injured area with her fingers, but now she looked up at Connie. 'The bag's in the hallway in the cupboard under the stairs. Would you go and fetch it for me?'

Connie nodded and shot off towards the hallway, while Rebecca and Angie did what they could to reassure the young man.

'Can you hear me, James?' Rebecca queried gently, recognizing the young medical student. 'Do you know what happened to you?'

James mumbled a reply and Rebecca guessed that a combination of alcohol and blood loss was causing him difficulty in responding. She said in a soothing voice, 'I want you to lie still while I try to control the bleeding. I'm going to raise your arm for a while to slow things down a bit, and then I'm going to bind a pressure pad in place on your arm. We need to get you to hospital so that your cuts can be stitched.'

By the time the paramedics arrived, she had things more or less under control. She made James as comfortable as possible and watched over his transfer to the ambulance, and it was only when the vehicle had moved off along the road that she made her way back inside the building.

She expected to find chaos still reigning, but most of the revellers were winding down and making ready to leave. Angie and Connie were making inroads on the clearing-up, and Craig was seeing to it that the remaining guests found safe transport home.

'I'll give you a hand in a minute or two,' she said to the girls. 'I just need to freshen up first.'

Rebecca went into the bathroom and rinsed her hands under the tap, then pulled a brush through the long swathe of her hair, staring at her reflection in the mirror. She gave a soft sigh. There were faint shadows beneath her eyes and her skin had a pale, translucent gleam. Would this day ever end? Her aunt was ill, her sister was still overseas, and her own carefully made travel plans had fallen apart when her little patient at the hospital had been too poorly to be transferred by ambulance to his original hospital. So far, it had turned out to be a kind of postscript to all that was going wrong in her life. None of her dreams had come to fruition in this place.

Her boyfriend, who had persuaded her to come here in the first instance, had cheated on her, and the work that she had believed would be so fulfilling, using her skills as a doctor to tend to desperately ill young patients on the paediatric ward, had brought her torment and sadness along with its rewards.

All in all, she would be glad to be away from here, to leave the hectic rush of the city behind her.

She started to exit the bathroom, pulling open the door, but before she made her way back to the living room she took a moment to lean back against the tiled wall, closing her eyes and pulling in a deep, calming breath. Was there any way this day could disintegrate any further?

'Are you all right?'

Craig's deep voice cut into her thoughts, eddying around her, coaxing a response, and she quickly opened her eyes. 'I'm fine,' she said.

His gaze was watchful. 'I thought you handled everything that happened back there really well.' There was a faint inflection in his voice as he added, 'You seemed to know what you were doing, and because of you your friend James will probably come through this all right.'

She looked at him. 'You sound as though you're surprised by that. It's not so incredible, is it?' She smiled lightly. 'I know it must have appeared to you as if things have been wildly out of control around here, but we all have to accept that there are times when everything that can go wrong does go wrong. It's just been one of those days where you get out of bed and wish you could have stayed under the covers.'

He nodded. His smoke grey glance travelled over her, sliding over the creamy slope of her bare shoulders and moving down to linger on the soft swell of her hips. 'I can see occasions when that might be an inviting prospect,' he said in a husky, amused drawl.

Rebecca pulled in a quick breath. She felt a rush of warm colour run along her cheekbones. Was he actually propositioning her? The way he was looking at her could hardly be misinterpreted, could it? And yet just a short time ago he had been treating her almost as though she was someone he would only have dealings with if he couldn't avoid it.

'Dream on,' she murmured, her mouth making a taut line. 'I may have been enjoying the party but I haven't had that much to drink.'

He laughed, a low rumbling sound that started in the back of his throat. 'Perhaps that's just as well,' he said. 'Your friend tells me you have to be at work early in the morning. Perhaps we'd both do best to keep a clear head.'

'You're probably right.' Rebecca pushed herself away from the wall. 'I'd better go and give Angie a hand with the clearing-up.' She sent him a quick glance. 'I should thank you for helping us out. We would have struggled without you.'

'I was glad to be able to do something.' He returned her gaze with a look that she couldn't quite interpret. Perhaps it was a mix between a threat and a promise because he added in a soft tone, 'Maybe I'll drop by in the morning and see if you're doing all right. You seem to have had a pretty traumatic day, one way and another.'

'I'll be fine,' she told him as she started towards the living room. 'I'll see you out. I expect you have things of your own that you need to be doing.'

He wasn't likely to find her at home by the time he surfaced, judging from his efforts this morning. She would be up and away first thing, ready to make the move to her Scottish island home. As far as she was concerned it couldn't come a minute too soon.

CHAPTER TWO

'I'LL miss you so much, Rebecca.' Angie put aside her coffee-cup and came across the kitchen to give her a hug. 'You have to promise me that you'll phone and let me know how you're getting on. You will, won't you? And maybe we could meet up again from time to time?'

'On high days and holidays? Of course…I'm not going to be all that far away—at least, not as the crow flies.' Rebecca smiled. After a few snatched hours of sleep, she was on much better form today. 'And I'll phone you as soon as I'm settled back in Scotland.'

'That's good. You'll have to let me know how you're getting on.' Angie's expression was wistful. 'I'll be thinking of you when you're on your island, looking out over the sea or walking along the beach. You're so lucky, being offered the chance to work there.'

'It sounds wonderful, doesn't it? Of course, the job isn't cut and dried yet, so I might have to look around for something temporary to tide me over. It all depends on whether the doctor at the centre changes her mind and decides that she might want to go back to work after her maternity leave—or whether I'll find it's not really what I'm looking for. At the moment, though, the prospect of working with mothers and babies in an island community seems ideal.'

'Just as long as it doesn't make you feel broody.' Angie grinned. 'All those babies would be bound to set me off… It's just a question of finding the right man…'

Rebecca wrinkled her nose. 'You'll manage that all right, but I don't think that's going to happen for me any time soon. I've already had my fingers burned and I'm not looking to get involved with anyone.'

'Ah, but Ben was a mistake. He seemed perfect for you to begin with, until he revealed his true colours, the ratfink. But there'll be someone out there, waiting for you, I'm sure of it.'

'Not if I see him first.' The words came out with a little more vehemence than Rebecca had intended, but she wasn't going to back down. 'I'm a long way from trusting any man ever again.'

Even her parents had managed to mess up their relationship, with consequences that had been devastating for Rebecca and her sister, Alison. Neither of them was going to recover easily from the distress of living through the break-up of their parents' marriage and the trauma of coming to terms with the chaos and uncertainty of a broken home.

She didn't have any faith that there was someone out there with whom she could find lasting happiness. No, she would definitely be better off keeping clear of the opposite sex while she licked her wounds.

'You're out of your mind.' Angie laughed. 'Everybody needs someone.' She rinsed her cup under the tap. 'I have to go. I have to review patients with the consultant before he does his ward round, and he's always there bright and early before the patients have even had their early morning cuppa.'

'That's because he likes to take breakfast with Sister Hennessy first thing. She keeps a stack of pancakes in the fridge and he's very partial to a toasted pancake with a drizzle of honey on it.'

'Really?' Angie's eyes widened. 'So that's why I see him coming out of her office most mornings. And there was me thinking they were sitting together having a case conference. Well, you live and learn, don't you?'

'You certainly do.' Rebecca gave her a hug and saw her out of the flat a few minutes later, waving as Angie turned at the door. 'I'll call you,' she said.

Once Angie had gone, Rebecca zipped up her suitcases and then walked desultorily around the flat, checking each of the rooms for any belongings that she might have missed. Just a few minutes from now she would be on her way, too.

The doorbell rang, and she went out into the lobby to answer it, wheeling her cases along with her. It would be the carrier, arriving to take her luggage to the depot, ready to be sent along to her new home.

'Are you off on a journey of some sort?' Craig Braemar was walking across the hallway as she headed for the door, and now he stopped and frowned, his gaze tracking her movements.

She stood very still. So he was still around, up and about early in the day, exactly as he had said he would be. Somehow she had expected him to be lying around, easing himself into the day. 'Just the cases, for the moment,' she said. 'I'll be following on later.'

He raised a dark brow. 'That sounds intriguing.'

'Maybe.' She saw that he had his overnight bag with him, and it prompted her to ask, 'And while we're on the subject, what about you? Are you leaving already? I've heard of people doing a moonlight flit, but the rent isn't that steep, is it?'

He appeared to be thinking about that. 'I wouldn't know,' he murmured. 'I haven't paid any.'

Rebecca gave him a long look. Why was it she could never tell whether he was joking or being serious?

So far, he wasn't turning out to be at all what he'd seemed, and it bothered her that she couldn't work him out. She decided to give up the attempt and concentrate her attention instead on the man who had come to collect her luggage.

She signed his paperwork, and checked that the destination was written clearly on his sheet. 'It's to go to Islay… you know that, right? I'd hate to get there and find everything has been mislaid.'

'Islay, madam. Yes, that's definitely what it says.'

'Hmm.' She looked at him and wondered whether she ought to hand him a tip. Perhaps to be on the safe side…

The man acknowledged her offering and retreated to his van.

Turning back into the hallway, she saw that Craig was watching her thoughtfully. 'Does this mean that you're off to see your aunt—the lady who was feeling unwell?'

'That's right. I rang her this morning and she said that she was fine and that everyone is making a fuss over nothing, but that's my Aunt Heather all over. She's always been an independent soul. I've been reluctant to interfere,

but it will be just as well for me to go and keep an eye on
her for a while.'

'I think that's a good idea. Down here, you're a long way
from being able to do anything to help. That's the trouble
with old folk, isn't it? They say they're all right because
they're afraid of being a burden, but sometimes you have
to read between the lines, don't you?'

A small spark of irritation flared in her eyes. Was he
implying that she hadn't been able to do that? What was it
to do with him, anyway?

'My aunt isn't all that old. At least, she doesn't seem to
be. She's always been active and energetic.' Why was he
so intent on wrongfooting her? She loved her aunt dearly,
but he didn't seem to be taking that on board.

She had to admit that he'd hit a sore spot, though. Right
from the start she'd had misgivings about leaving her home
to go and work in Northumberland with her boyfriend. It
had only been Ben's enthusiasm and gentle insistence that
had convinced her it had been the thing to do.

'It'll be wonderful,' he had said. 'You'll be able to work
in paediatrics, and I'll take on the research fellowship. We
could buy a house close to the hospital, and it'll be great
for both of us.'

The doubts had stayed with her, firstly because she had
been worried about leaving Aunt Heather behind, despite
the fact that her sister was going to be staying around to
watch over her for some of the time, and secondly because
she had been uncertain about moving in with Ben.

She'd thought he had been the one for her, but after all
was said and done, he hadn't offered her total commitment,
had he? Just an arrangement that had been convenient.

And so she had resisted the temptation to move in with him, and that had proved to be a wise decision, hadn't it, given the way things had turned out?

'I've kept in touch with my aunt while I've been away,' she said now. 'And I've been home to see her a few times. It's not as though she's been abandoned.'

Craig studied her, a flicker of scepticism in his expression. 'You don't have to convince me,' he said. 'She's not my aunt, so it hardly matters to me. I just happened to remark that it looks as though you must have decided to go back to her.'

'Yes, well, that's true, I have.' She frowned. 'There are actually lots of things that I need to do, and I ought to leave right now,' she told him. 'I'm due at the hospital in twenty minutes.'

He nodded. 'Me, too. We could walk there together, if you like.'

She frowned, taken aback by what he had just said. He'd only stayed here for two nights, and now he was off to the hospital with his overnight bag. Was it possible that she had added two and two together and come up with the wrong answer? Was he ill? Had she completely misjudged him?

She looked again at the bag he was holding. 'Are you going to be staying at the hospital?' she asked. He looked as though he was in perfect health, in the prime of his life, in fact, a thirtysomething example of vigorous masculinity, but that didn't necessarily have to mean that he didn't need treatment of some kind, did it? A warm flood of guilt raced through her from head to toe.

'No,' he answered slowly. 'I wouldn't have thought I

would be there for too long. Just the time it takes to sort things out.'

'I'm sorry—of course it's none of my business.' It was dreadful to think that she might have been imagining him as some kind of drifter when all the time he was ill and preparing for a stay in hospital.

He looked at her in a slightly perplexed fashion for a moment or two and then opened his mouth as though he was about to say something, but she swivelled around and headed for the door of her flat, saying hurriedly, 'I'll just go and check that everything's in order before I lock the place up. Then I'll be ready to walk with you.'

She was back by his side within a moment or two, and they left the building together.

The block of flats was a ten-minute walk away from the hospital where she had worked for the last couple of years, and now, as she shut the main door behind her for the last time, she looked back with a feeling of sadness mingled with expectation. The island home of her youth beckoned her, but at the same time she was leaving behind friends and colleagues, and that was a painful experience.

'How is it that you have to go in to work if you're all set to leave here?' he asked as they set out along the street. 'Presumably you're travelling later today? I dare say there aren't many people who would be able to cope without their luggage for very long.'

'I have to transport an eight-year-old patient back home to Scotland. He was brought down here to Northumberland for specialist treatment after he was badly injured in a road accident, but now he's well enough to be transferred back to his local hospital. He was supposed to have gone yesterday by ambulance, but we were concerned about his condition and so we delayed things for a while.'

'So it wasn't necessary for you to wait to go with him? You could have left it to someone else to escort him?'

She made a face. 'I suppose that's true, but I've been looking after him for a while now, overseeing his care, and he wanted me to stay with him. It's been a difficult time for Connor, because his parents were injured in the crash as well and they had to stay behind in Scotland. I think that's why he took to depending on me, because he was so vulnerable. The poor child had no one and he was lost and alone.'

'Then I expect you must feel that you made the right choice.' He sent her an oblique glance. 'So, what do you do at the hospital? Are you a nurse, or a doctor perhaps?'

'A doctor. I specialised in paediatrics, and mostly I work with seriously ill children on the surgical ward.'

'That must be rewarding.' His blue-grey gaze moved over her fleetingly.

'It can be. There are times when it's difficult to handle, though, like when the child has a serious heart condition or worse. You want so much to help them, but sometimes there's a limit to what you can do. I find that heartbreaking.'

He nodded. 'I can see how that might affect you. For myself, I tend to think that children are resilient for the most part. They cope with problems in a way that puts adults to shame.'

Rebecca smiled. 'Yes, they do.' She sent him a thoughtful glance. She knew next to nothing about this man, and yet he already had the lowdown on her lifestyle, her work and her plans for the future. Well, maybe not all of them, but a good part. How had he managed to glean so much about her in such a short space of time?

'Here we are already,' he said as the glass doors to the main entrance of the hospital swished open before them. 'That was quick. You certainly landed a prime position, with your flat being just a hop and a skip away from here.'

'I suppose I did.' Rebecca hesitated, and then started to move away from him in the direction of the stairs. 'I have to go to the surgical ward to collect my patient,' she told him. 'Do you know your way about, or do you need directions?'

'I'll manage,' he murmured. 'I'll take the lift.'

'OK.'

He inclined his head towards her and she returned the gesture with a brief 'Goodbye,' before going on her way.

She didn't turn back to watch him take the lift. She wouldn't be seeing him again and that was perhaps just as well, because he seemed to have a very strange effect on her. In the few hours she had known him, he had managed somehow to put her on the defensive and caused her to examine her reasons for doing things, and she was tired of all that uncertainty.

What she needed now was a fresh start, a chance to go home to her island roots and find peace within herself once again.

Pushing all thoughts of him out of her mind, she tapped in the security code at the door of the children's ward and then made her way over to the nurses' station.

'How's everybody doing?' she asked, looking at the

women who had been her colleagues over the last couple of years. 'Has everything been peaceful overnight?'

'More peaceful than your going-away party.' Connie laughed. 'Have you heard any news about James?'

Rebecca nodded. 'I checked up on him by phone before I came here. He's doing all right… He had several deep cuts that needed stitching, but he's recovering well, and they're thinking of sending him home later today.'

'That's a relief.' Connie smiled. 'As to your little patient, he's just about ready for the journey home. He's a bit pale and anxious-looking, but his temperature is OK and his heart rate and oxygen levels are satisfactory, so he should be clear to travel.'

'That's good news. I'll go and have a word with him and get him ready for the journey. Do we have any idea what time the ambulance will be arriving?'

Connie glanced at the nurse who was standing by the phone. 'Do we?'

'I'm not sure. I think we have to check with the transport services. There was a query over what was happening, and I was told to ring again in a few minutes to check.'

'That's all right. I'll go and talk to Connor while you do that.'

Eight-year-old Connor was overjoyed to see her. 'Becca, you came back!' Her young patient's face lit up. 'I know you said you were going to stay with me, but they told me you weren't going to work at the hospital any more. I didn't think I would see you again.'

'Well, there you are, you see,' she said on a cheerful note. 'I'm here, and I'm going with you all the way back to Scotland. I shan't leave you until I hand you over, safe and sound, to your mum and dad.'

He gave her a blissful smile. 'I can't wait to see them again.' He sank back against his pillows as though the effort of talking had taken a lot out of him. Even so, he shot her a troubled glance. 'Do you think they're all right? Are they still in hospital?'

She nodded. 'They're both still in hospital, but they're getting better every day.' His mother had leg and arm injuries, and his father was suffering from whiplash and a dislocated knee, but Connor was the one who had come close to death because of internal injuries.

She looked at him now, noting the dark shadows beneath his eyes, made all the more noticeable by his pale features and the contrasting colour of his brown hair. He had lost a lot of blood in the car accident, and had almost died from injuries to his chest and abdomen. It was only because of the skill of the surgeons who had operated on him within the golden hour, from the time of the accident to admission to hospital, that he stood a good chance of recovery without suffering too many after-effects. In fact, all going well, he would probably be released from hospital in a few days.

'We need to concentrate on you right now,' she murmured. 'We have to make sure that you're well enough to manage the journey, and that you stay on good form. That means you need to get some rest and allow your body to heal. We still need to keep an eye on you to make sure that everything gets back to normal.'

'I'm better than I was yesterday.' Connor gave her a wide-eyed glance. 'And I ate all my breakfast, even the yucky porridge the nurse gave me.'

Rebecca laughed. 'That's good. It's a start, at any rate.' She surreptitiously checked the readings on the monitors by his bedside. 'I'll have a quick listen to your chest, and then perhaps we can get ready to go on our way.'

She gently laid her stethoscope over his rib cage and listened to the sounds coming from his lungs. There was a slight wheeziness, but all in all things appeared to be good. Since the drainage tubes had been removed from his chest a couple of days ago with no ill-effects, it looked as though she could give the all-clear for the transport to go ahead.

'You're doing all right,' she told him with a smile, 'so I'll go and have a word with the nurse and see if we can be on our way.'

'Yeah!' Connor whooped, and then coughed, clutching his chest as his body responded to the exertion. 'Ouch!' he said. 'That hurt.'

Rebecca made a wry face. 'I guess we'd better top up your painkillers before we go.' She reached into her pocket and pulled out an electronic computer game. 'Here, you can amuse yourself with this for a while, if you think you're up to it.'

'Oh, wow.' His eyes shone as he looked up at her. 'Where did you get this from?'

'I borrowed it from the play leader. She didn't want you to be bored on the journey.'

He was already thumbing the buttons on the device, absorbed in checking out the game she had slotted in place. 'This is great.'

Rebecca grinned, and went off to talk to the nurse. 'How are things coming along with the transport?' she asked.

'You're all set to go,' the nurse told her. 'Only there

won't be a paramedic travelling along with you this time. There will be another doctor on board.'

'That's unusual, isn't it?' Rebecca murmured. 'How did that come about?'

'I think it was because— Oh, hang on, here he is now…' The nurse broke off and looked towards the door. 'He'll be able to fill you in on the details himself.' She shielded her face with her hand in a covert fashion as she turned back to Rebecca. 'Lucky you! I wish I were the one who was going along with him. He's gorgeous.'

Rebecca's stare flicked across the room and she gazed in open-mouthed wonder at the man who was walking towards them. She blinked in disbelief. Surely there was some mistake? What was Craig doing there? How was it possible that the nurse was pointing him out as though he was the doctor who was to accompany her on the journey?

Craig's dark brows lifted. 'Are you all right?' He came to join them at the nurses' station, sending Rebecca a swift, assessing glance. 'You look as though you're in shock.'

'I think that's because I am.' Rebecca floundered. 'I mean, I had no idea that you were anything other than a stranger passing through. How was I to know that you were a doctor? You didn't tell me.'

His gaze was steady. 'You didn't ask.'

'Yes, but even so…' Rebecca shook her head. All her preconceived ideas about him had dissolved in an instant. To think that she had even been feeling some degree of sympathy towards him…and now it turned out that she had everything wrong and she felt utterly foolish.

'I had no idea that you would be going back with me to

Scotland,' she said. 'You must have known all along, but
you said nothing at all.'

'That's because I didn't know for certain,' he murmured.
'I had a shrewd idea, I'll grant you, but I knew nothing for
sure until I checked with the transport services a few
minutes ago.'

He looked across at the nurse. 'So we're cleared to go,
I take it? Where is the little fellow?'

'Bay three.' The nurse pointed in the direction of the side
ward, an amused smile playing around her lips. 'I have his
paperwork here, all ready for Dr McIntyre. I hope you
both have a good journey.'

Rebecca drew in a swift breath and put out a hand for
the paperwork. She would at least put up a semblance of
normality and pretend that none of this was happening.
'Thanks,' she said. 'I'll make sure it's handed over to the
receiving hospital. It's been good working with you,
Libby.'

'And you.'

Rebecca started towards the bay where Connor was
waiting. 'I'll show you to our patient,' she told Craig. Perhaps the best thing she could do was to relate to him in a
purely professional capacity. That way, she would be able
to stay calm and do her job. 'He's doing all right,' she said.
'It's just a question of waiting for him to heal and for him
to build up his strength once more. All this has taken a lot
out of him.'

'I can imagine.'

He was still carrying the overnight bag with him, and
she said briskly as they approached Connor's trolley bed,
'Perhaps you should slide that onto the rack underneath.

It'll be out of the way as we wheel him out to the ambulance bay.'

'Sure thing.' He deposited the bag and sent a cheery smile towards Connor, who was looking at him with a guarded expression. 'Hello, young man,' Craig said. 'I'm Dr Braemar. I'll be going along with you on the journey home.'

Connor sent him a suspicious look. 'I want Becca to go with me.'

'Yes, she'll be coming along, too.'

'Really?' Connor lay back and tried to absorb that. 'So I get to have two doctors? Why?'

'That's a good question,' Craig said. 'The reason is, I came down here with a patient, but there were problems with the transport, and I had to stay over until they were fixed. So now I get to travel home with you and your delicious Dr McIntyre.' He leaned forward and gave the boy a clandestine, questioning look. 'You weren't hoping to keep her all to yourself, were you? 'Cos if you were, that means I'm stranded here, and I won't get back to Scotland in time to walk my dog.'

'You have a dog?'

Craig made a face. 'Actually, no. You found me out. I made it up, because I just wanted to make sure I get to go with you.'

Connor chuckled. 'You're crackers.'

Craig grinned. 'Yeah. So they keep telling me.'

Rebecca could think of a few more adjectives to describe him. Words like underhand, annoying and in your face all sprang to mind.

'Are you all set to go?' she asked Connor, and the boy

nodded. 'Good. Then we'll move you out to the lift and take you down to the ambulance bay.'

'Um…' Craig looked as though he was about to say something, but Rebecca was already releasing the brake on the bed and he nimbly stepped to one side as she set the bed in motion. 'Was there something you wanted to say?' she queried, shooting him a quick glance.

'It'll wait,' he said, grimacing as she set off towards the exit door. 'Far be it from me to disturb a woman while she's driving.'

Connor giggled, and Rebecca sent Craig a warning glare. Was he looking for trouble?

She waved goodbye to her friends as she left, and then, when she was outside in the main corridor, she headed for the lifts. She steered the boy through the open lift doors and put a hand out to press the button to send them on their way. 'Going down,' she told Connor, but just as she was about to choose the ground-floor switch, Craig intervened.

'In fact,' he said, 'we need to go up…to the top floor.' He pressed the button for the roof area and the doors silently closed on them.

She stared at him. 'Why on earth would we need to do that?'

'Because that's where the helipad is.'

'Oh, fantastic,' Connor said. 'Do we really get to go in a helicopter?'

'That's right. It's the only way to travel.'

'Excuse me?' Rebecca was still trying to absorb the shock. She half turned so that Connor would not be able to see or hear what she was about to say, and Craig must have read the warning signals in her expression because he gave her his full attention.

'This can't be right,' she said in a low tone. 'No one said anything to me about a helicopter.' She felt the colour wash out of her face.

'It was just how things turned out, that's all. I have to go back up north, and so do you and Connor, so it makes sense for us all to travel together, doesn't it?' He stopped suddenly, taking in her pale features. 'Why, is there a problem?'

'No, of course not,' she lied through her teeth. How could she possibly voice her true thoughts with Connor beside her? 'Why would there be?'

Craig put his head to one side as though he was trying to assess what was going through her mind. 'You're used to flying, aren't you? Living on Islay, I dare say you would find it the best way to travel.'

The lift came to a halt before she had time to answer, and the doors opened out on to the roof space, so that a gust of fresh air met them. Rebecca looked out to see the brightly painted helicopter, ready and waiting on the helipad, its rotors turning.

She patted the blankets in place around Connor to make him snug, but after that she stayed rooted to the spot, so Craig took over the handling of the trolley bed and someone who introduced himself as the copilot came over to greet them.

'I'll give you a hand getting the patient on board,' he told Craig, stopping for a moment to greet Connor. 'We'll soon have you tucked up cosy as you like.'

Connor nodded, and turned his head to look at Rebecca.

'You're coming, aren't you, Becca? You said you would.' His face was pale, and she realised that even this small excitement had been enough to tire him out.

'Yes, I did. Of course I did.' She ventured forward a few steps to give him encouragement and then stood still. 'I'll just wait here for a moment while they get you on board.'

Craig came to find her when the child was settled inside the cabin. 'Are you ready?' he asked.

'No, I don't think so,' she said. She looked at him. 'I don't do helicopter rides. I tried one once and told myself never again. You should have warned me. Someone should have told me.'

'There's nothing to it,' he said. 'Helicopters take off day in, day out. The sky is clear, and we're all set to go. What could go wrong?'

'You tell me,' she said abruptly. 'You were the one who said you had to stay over while your transport was fixed.' She looked him in the eye. 'That means there was a problem, right?'

His shoulders lifted in a negligent shrug. 'It was nothing. Just a faint judder in the engine. But they've checked it out and everything's fine.'

'No, I don't think it is. Everything is not fine, far from it. No one told me about this and I'm finding it hard to take in.'

'You'll only be up there for half an hour…an hour at the most,' he said. He moved closer to her and placed an arm around her shoulders, drawing her against his chest. 'I'll sit with you and hold your hand if you like.' He pulled an exaggeratedly fiendish face, halfway between a leer and a smile, and Rebecca balled her hand into a fist and thumped him lightly in the arm.

'This is not funny. It's not at all funny.' She was battling with herself, trying to shake off the nerves that threatened to overwhelm her. At the same time she was trying not to think about the way it felt to have his arm draped about her, drawing her into the warmth and shelter of his body. She would not be enticed by the comfort of that embrace.

It was a sham, a pretence set up to fool her into complying with what he wanted her to do.

Like Angie had said of her ex-boyfriend, he was a ratfink. None of them were to be trusted.

CHAPTER THREE

'YOU'LL be fine,' Craig told Rebecca. 'I promise you. Anyway,' he added, 'it's a twin-engined aircraft, and it's regularly maintained so that you can rely on it to give top performance and ensure your comfort at the same time. Honestly, there's nothing at all for you to worry about.'

'I've heard all that before,' Rebecca muttered. 'Besides, you sound like an advertisement for the helicopter company. I'll have you know that the last time I flew in one of those contraptions the machine developed a tail rotor failure and the pilot had to make a difficult landing. It was scary, to say the least. Believe me, it isn't something I'd like to go through again.'

Even now, some years later, she could recall the way the passengers had been thrown about from side to side as the pilot had tried to keep control of the machine. They had been strapped securely in their seats, but she'd borne the bruises from the restraints across her chest for some time afterwards. That was the least of her worries, though. It was the thought of what might have been that bothered her most.

Craig put on a serious expression. 'I can see how you

wouldn't want to do that, but nothing bad is going to happen, is it? Lightning doesn't strike twice, and anyway, when all's said and done, the pilot landed you safely last time, didn't he? They're trained to cope in all sorts of circumstances. Believe me, you have nothing to worry about.'

Her gaze narrowed on him. He would say that, wouldn't he? He was as exuberant and fired up as though there was nothing more to it than climbing on a bus. Nothing seemed to jar his confidence, whereas she was still fighting with herself, trying to come to terms with this new shock to her system.

'You can't possibly understand,' she said. 'You have absolutely no idea how I feel about this.'

He shrugged. 'Maybe not,' he said, 'but I do know that life is for living and sometimes you have to take chances, otherwise you would do nothing but sit and quiver in a corner and wonder about what might have been.'

Rebecca scowled. He probably thought she was a complete wimp, but what did he know of how she had struggled to come to terms with what had happened before?

In the end, though, what choice did she have in this situation? Connor was relying on her to stay with him throughout this journey, and she couldn't let him down, could she? He was just a young boy who was sick and dependent on her. He had already been through more in his young life than any child should suffer. How would she live with herself if she went back on her word?

With that solely in mind, she straightened her shoulders and began to walk towards the helicopter, well aware that Craig was staying close by her side the whole time. Perhaps he was afraid that she would change her mind and decide to turn back.

Once inside the helicopter, Rebecca tried to put aside her fears and busied herself by going to check on Connor. She took no notice at all of what Craig might be doing.

'How are you bearing up?' she asked the child as she made sure that his safety harness was fixed securely in position.

'I'm OK.' The boy mumbled, already half-asleep, and for a few moments afterwards his breathing appeared to be slightly laboured. He looked as though he was exhausted.

She checked the portable monitors. His heart rate had increased and there was a slight flush to his cheeks, but perhaps both of those things were only to be expected, given the nature of the journey ahead. His temperature was slightly raised, but there was nothing that she could see that would give her cause for concern.

'You should make sure that you're strapped in,' the copilot advised her, 'and then we can be on our way.'

She nodded, acknowledging him and the pilot, a man in his late thirties, who gave a brief wave of his hand before turning back to check his instrument panel. Rebecca looked around at the seating area and then chose a position where she would easily be able to attend to Connor throughout the flight.

In the meantime, Craig slipped a headset in place over the boy's ears and then went to find his own seat nearby. He fastened his safety harness and checked that she had done the same.

'Put on your headset,' he told her. 'It will be easier for us to talk to one another that way.' He indicated a switch that enabled two-way communication, and she nodded to show that she understood.

'He seems to be coping fairly well so far,' he said, giving a slight nod towards Connor. 'With any luck we'll have him settled in the hospital back home before too long. I gather his parents are on the mend and waiting to see him?'

'That's right. They've been keeping in touch, of course, by phone. I rang the hospital this morning, and the staff nurse said that both of them were doing reasonably well. His father's had an operation to fix his damaged knee, and Connor's mother is up and about now, although she's having to rely on crutches.'

'That's good. I expect it will have cheered Connor up to know that his parents are doing all right.'

Rebecca nodded, but her concentration began to waver as the pilot put the helicopter in motion, and she felt the pull of being lifted up into the air. A huge knot started to form in her stomach. For a moment or two she felt nauseous, and after a while she realised that she was gripping the arm of her seat so tightly that her knuckles were turning white.

She tried breathing in deeply for a while, but it didn't seem to be having much of an effect. Pulling a tissue from her pocket, she dabbed at the clammy beads of perspiration that had started to form on her brow.

'We'll be going over Kielder Water very soon,' Craig said. 'You can already see the moorland and the pine forests coming into view. Keep watching and you'll see that there's a lovely hotel just beyond the lake. It'll come into view any minute now. It's a great starting point from there to explore the Chevin Hills and the woodland all around.'

Rebecca was trying to listen to what he was saying, but her heart was thumping in an erratic fashion, and she was finding it difficult to stay in control of herself. She had to get a grip on her emotions, because she was there first and foremost to watch over her patient, and what use would she be to him if she let her nerves get the better of her?

'Take a look out of the window,' Craig urged. He leaned across her, his chest brushing her arm as he moved to show her the view. 'See, over there,' he murmured. 'There's a beautiful log cabin, nestled among the silver birch trees. I've stayed there, it's fabulous. There's a veranda, where you can sit on a hammock and watch the sun sink below the horizon.'

He glanced down at her, a glimmer of teasing invitation in his eyes. 'You should try it some time. There can't be anything more satisfying than to simply laze away a summer's evening with nothing more to do than snack on good food and sip cocktails.'

It might well be a pleasant prospect, but Rebecca was in no state to take in his advice. In fact, she was doing her utmost to try to ignore the way his arm almost wrapped itself around her as he pointed out the distant hills. It set off alarm bells in her head, and her heart, still pounding from the anxiety of take-off, increased its beat to a staccato, heavy thud.

Maybe it wouldn't be such a bad idea to think about that log cabin for a while. At the least it might help to calm her down. The very image of a log cabin conjured up woodland scenes, fishing by the lake and long walks in the countryside.

Who had joined him on those walks? Of course, she didn't imagine for a moment that he would have been there alone. Her brow furrowed. And why should that thought bother her, anyway? She hardly knew the man, and yet even now when she was at her most vulnerable state he had managed to permeate her consciousness and stir her curiosity.

Her mouth made a wry twist. 'Chance would be a fine thing,' she said, 'but I imagine you must have an affinity for that kind of leisure activity.'

Keyed up as she was, she regretted the words almost as soon as she had said them. After all, he might have come across as a kind of happy-go-lucky vagrant initially, but in reality he was nothing of the sort. It was only her heightened sense of apprehension that was making her so crabby and ill mannered.

He laughed. 'Don't we all?' He sent her a fleeting glance. 'Be honest, would you still be doing this job if you could swap places with a millionaire playboy?'

'Probably,' she said, her tone short. 'There is a certain satisfaction in knowing that you're saving lives and helping people to recover from unfortunate events, don't you think?'

He gave a noncommittal shrug, as though he might be sceptical about that, and she frowned. Was he really as indifferent as he appeared? All her life she had wanted to be a doctor, to be able to take care of people in their hour of need. No matter what setbacks and dilemmas she had come up against in her career, none of that had ever changed.

She looked over to where Connor lay, casting a sweeping glance over the monitors. The child's breathing was becoming more laboured and his oxygen level was gradually falling.

She unhooked the oxygen equipment from its mounting and, raising him lightly, showed Connor the breathing mask. 'This will help to ease your chest,' she told the boy. 'I'm just going to place it over your nose. Try breathing in as deeply as you can.'

Connor did as she suggested, and after a while Rebecca began to relax a little as his oxygen level began to rise slightly.

Satisfied that she had done everything she could for the moment, she settled back in her seat. Or rather she tried to settle. There was no escaping the fact that they were still hurtling through the air, the rotors whirring above them, and far below her the landscape stretched out for miles around in all directions.

'We're heading towards the southern uplands,' Craig said. 'If you look closely, you might be able to see eagles nesting on the high crags.' He pointed over to her left. 'Sometimes, if you're lucky, you might catch a glimpse of one of them soaring through the sky.'

Rebecca gave a small shudder. 'I think I prefer not to do that,' she said. It would mean she had to look out over that broad sweep of land so far below. 'I don't believe my stomach could take it.'

Despite her words, though, she couldn't help but let her gaze follow where he pointed, and what she saw was stunning. There were rolling hills and deep valleys, broken by occasional outcrops of rock, and as the helicopter began to veer to the left, heading in a north-westerly direction, the sight of the shimmering lochs took her breath away. It was beautiful, but when she looked more carefully, she could see that the water glistened and churned restlessly, whipped up by blustery air currents that eddied all around.

Rebecca frowned. When had the wind suddenly started up? When they had started out the sky had been relatively clear, helping to ease away some of the doubts she had about taking this flight. Now, though, things weren't looking quite so calm. There were clouds up ahead, and the sky was turning grey.

'Are those stormclouds gathering?' she asked in a low voice. She was almost thinking aloud, but Craig had picked up her words through his headset.

'It's just a bit of bad weather coming our way.' He confirmed her uneasy thoughts, but didn't seem at all bothered by the change in the weather. 'I expect the pilot will try to go around it. That's probably why we're heading toward the coast.'

He hadn't eased back from her at all, and for the most part he appeared to be intent on watching the landscape beneath them. Rebecca tried to focus her attention on the unfolding scene. It was either that or take note of the way his body was leaning against hers, and that would have been far too distracting for her peace of mind. He was so close to her that she felt the warmth emanating from his skin, and she could almost imagine how it might be if he was to lay his cheek against hers. Just the thought of that happening was enough to send her body into sizzling reaction.

'Perhaps you should give me a little space,' she murmured after a while. 'I need to take a look at Connor. I've a feeling his chest is giving him trouble.'

Craig moved back in an instant, and suddenly Rebecca found herself missing that close contact. She sent him a surreptitious glance, and found that he was watching her closely, a quizzical expression playing about his lips.

That expression made her pause and question what was going on. Had all his actions been quite deliberate from the outset? The thought struck her as she turned to survey the monitors. Every moment that she had battled with the feeling his nearness stirred up in her had been one less moment in time when she might have worried about the hazards of the flight.

Connor stirred, drawing her attention to him. 'How are you feeling?' she asked softly.

The boy didn't answer. His eyes were open but his breathing was shallow and fast and she realised that his condition was beginning to deteriorate. 'Is it your chest that's bothering you?' she asked.

He nodded, and tried to say something, but she forestalled him. 'It's all right. I understand. I think you may have some fluid on your lungs that is causing you to have some problems with your breathing. I'm going to give you some medicine that should help to clear up any infection that might be starting up. It'll take just a little while to work, but you should start to feel more comfortable before too long.'

There was too much turbulence for her to safely prepare an injection, so she relied on giving him the antibiotic, together with a painkiller and sedative, by mouth. Just as she was getting him to sip it down, she heard the pilot say,

'We've run into squally conditions, so you all need to pre-pare yourselves for a bit of a bumpy ride.'

Connor looked alarmed, and despite her own inner qualms she patted his hand and said, 'It's all right, sweet-heart. There's nothing to worry about. It'll be a bit like a fairground ride. I don't suppose it will last for all that long, though, because we can't be too far away from home now. I expect your mum and dad are waiting impatiently. They must be looking forward to seeing you again.'

A faint smile crossed his mouth. 'Yes,' he managed on a breathy sigh.

Rebecca watched him close his eyes, and then she sent a swift glance in Craig's direction. He had gathered up a kit box, placing it in close proximity to his seat, and he was checking out the positioning of the medical equipment about the cabin.

For a moment she wondered if he might be planning ahead in case some kind of emergency developed with their small patient.

Then the helicopter made a sideways dive and the pilot had to manhandle the controls to bring it back on a level. The copilot was focusing his gaze on the instrument panel, and when she looked back at Craig she saw that he was turning his attention to the doors.

The pilot had called Flight Control. His voice was calm. 'I'm attempting to fly around the storm,' he said. 'The wind is increasing, and there are thunderclouds up ahead. I'm having trouble maintaining height and speed.'

The helicopter lurched once again, throwing them to one side, and Rebecca pulled in a quick breath. Craig's glance meshed with hers. 'How is the boy doing?' he asked.

'He's not too good right now. I think there must be some kind of infection building up in the pleural cavity,' she said. 'It's making it painful for him to breathe, so I've giving him a painkiller along with a strong antibiotic. I added a small dose of sedative, too, so I'm hoping he'll fall asleep again.'

Craig looked at Connor and nodded. 'It looks as though he might do that fairly soon.'

Rebecca lifted her medical bag and began to cram into it all the extra supplies she could reach from the helicopter's storage bay without having to leave her seat. Her heart was thudding with apprehension from the wild, bucking movements that the helicopter was making when all of a sudden the machine appeared to go into a dive and then recovered as the pilot battled to keep them on course. 'Is there any way we can safeguard the stretcher?' she asked.

'How do you mean?' Craig studied her thoughtfully, and she responded with a tight stare.

'I mean, is there any sort of flotation device that we can use to protect him in case we have to make an unscheduled landing?' she said. 'I can see perfectly well what's happening. I'm not a fool, and I've been here before, remember? Not in this place, but in this sort of situation.' She took a deep breath. 'I know why we're heading towards the coast. I knew all along that it was a mistake to believe you when you said that lightning doesn't strike twice.'

'There's a good chance that we'll be able to get around this,' he murmured, 'but you're right, it would be a good idea to get into lifejackets. Just as a precaution, you understand?'

Rebecca gritted her teeth. 'Like I said, I understand the

situation precisely.' She should never have allowed him to override her better judgement, should she? Right from the start she ought to have found some way of ensuring that Connor was transferred to the hospital by road as had originally been planned.

The copilot was obviously thinking along the same lines as them, because he turned and signalled that they should retrieve the lifejackets from the storage compartment.

'What about the stretcher? Is there something we can do to make it safe?'

'I'll have a look.' The copilot was out of his seat by now, wrestling with the latch of a locked compartment built into the wall of the cabin while he braved the erratic movements of the helicopter.

Craig unclipped his seat belt. 'I'll give you a hand, Tom.' The man nodded, and together the two men struggled to slide a protective covering around the child's stretcher. 'I think that's about the best we can do for now,' Tom murmured.

'You should get yourselves strapped in,' the pilot called out in an urgent tone. 'The storm is getting worse and I'm having trouble with the controls. They're not responding. Tom, I need you to come and give me a hand.'

'Will do.' Tom battled against the heaving motion of the helicopter, gaining handholds where he could as he made his way back to the controls. Rebecca watched anxiously as Craig stumbled towards his seat.

'Hurry,' she said. 'Fasten your safety belt.'

He slid into position beside her and she managed a small sigh of relief as he clamped the belt in place.

'There's no way I'm going to be able to keep this

machine in the air,' the pilot said. 'We're coming up to the mouth of the river, and I'm going to have to try to ditch the plane. Get ready to assume crash positions—we'll be making a nosedive, but I'll do my best to pull us up. The procedure is similar to how you would react in a fixed-wing aircraft—put your feet firmly on the floor, either directly in line with your knees or slightly forward. Bend forward at the waist and brace yourselves for impact.'

Rebecca did as she was told, but as she bent forward in her seat she felt Craig reach out to her. He placed the palm of his hand over her head and neck, keeping her pinned down, and she guessed that he was doing his best to prevent her from suffering any kind of neck injury.

Up front, the pilot was making a Mayday call, and it occurred to her that they were in a life-and-death situation together and she didn't even know his name.

As they rushed towards the ground, though, her thoughts were centred on the little boy who had been entrusted to her safekeeping. Would he survive this? How would the two men at the front of the plane fare when they made impact with the water? Would they make it that far, or would they all simply hurtle to the ground? Who would look after Aunt Heather if anything happened to her?

And then, in a brief, calm moment, she thought about Craig and the way he was trying to protect her. From the very start of this journey he had been trying to distract her and keep her mind off what might or might not come to pass. He had very nearly succeeded in that, and now all she could think about was how she had never actually managed to figure him out. What kind of man was he? What made him tick? Was he a lackadaisical, live-for-the-moment kind of man?

Suddenly there was an almighty thump, followed by a horrible grinding sound, and Rebecca instinctively reached for the stretcher, curling her hand around the sidebar and gripping it with all her might. The force of the impact jarred her whole body, sending shock waves reverberating all along her spine.

It seemed to her as though the helicopter was racing along the hard-packed earth for what seemed like an eternity. The sound of grinding metal screamed in her ears, the stretcher was wrenched from her hand and after that everything faded into a black abyss.

CHAPTER FOUR

REBECCA'S head was aching. Something was wrong, very wrong, she was sure of that. Yet, strangely, there was no noise, only a peculiar stillness that pervaded the atmosphere, and she had no idea where she was or what she had been doing up to this moment. Had she been going somewhere?

Her feet were wet. In fact, come to think of it, the whole of her lower body was soaked by ice-cold water...water that was beginning to move, drifting around her. Now, that was very odd. How could that be?

'We have to shut off the battery and fuel switches.' It was a ragged voice that she scarcely recognised, and above all it sounded as though whoever was talking was having great difficulty in getting the words out.

'Are all the doors free?' This person obviously needed to make sure that these matters were attended to because even though his tone was strained there was a note of urgency about it.

'They're OK on this side. I'm going to try and get you out of there, Tom, but you'll need to slide your legs out from under the panel for me. Do you think you can you do that?'

Now, there was a voice that she did recognise. Cool, calm and collected, a perfect foil for the desperate tones of the other man. She had always wondered how that would sound, and Craig's voice was a faultless example.

Hadn't Craig been holding onto her just a moment ago? She remembered that his hand had been at the back of her head, and his hold on her had been firm and wonderfully comforting…because they were in danger, and they were heading for disaster… Realisation dawned on her with a jolt. They had been about to crash, hadn't they?

Rebecca lifted her head. It hurt to do that, and she winced as the movement jarred. Her arm was sore, and she moved it experimentally, checking to see if it worked properly. It was OK. She was still in one piece.

Another thought struck her. Where was the stretcher? Where was Connor? Concerned now, she scanned the interior of the cabin and saw that the stretcher was behind her. The force of the landing must have thrown it backwards, wrenching it from the stanchions that were meant to hold it in place.

Connor was still strapped to the stretcher. His eyes were open, and he was staring about him.

She released the seat belt that was holding her, and then moved groggily to go and check on him, wading through the water that was steadily filling the cabin. She started to shiver. 'How are you doing?' she asked. 'Are you in pain?'

'My chest hurts,' he said in a low voice. 'I think I was asleep.' His breathing was laboured, and his cheeks were flushed with fever, but Rebecca couldn't see anything else that might be wrong with him, no damage that might have been caused by the crash. He was above the water level, the stretcher having come to rest on a container of some sort that was built into the side of the helicopter.

'Are we there yet?' he asked.

'Not yet, sweetheart.'

She glanced towards the front of the machine and saw that Craig was starting towards her. He looked unharmed, and that made her heart lift a little. 'How is the pilot?' she asked.

'He's slipping in and out of consciousness. I think he must have hit his head on one of the panels.' He looked her over. 'Are you injured in any way? When I looked at you a minute ago, you were quite dazed.'

'No, I'm fine.'

'That's good.' Even so, he threw her a second glance as though he was uncertain whether to believe her, and then he reached for her, preparing to help her out of the cabin. 'Take my hand. We need to move out of here. The whole thing is unstable.'

'Are we sinking? Are we going to be able to get the stretcher out?' She tried to see what was outside the helicopter, but they must have been tipped to one side because all she could see was the sky. 'How deep is the water out there?'

'I don't think it's too bad. We seem to be fairly close to the water's edge, so with a bit of luck we'll be able to wade to the bank of the river.'

Rebecca looked around for her medical kit, and then realised that she must have slipped the handle of the bag over her head before the crash, because it was still in place.

She felt peculiar. It was as though everything was happening in slow motion. She was trying to think about what she needed to do, but her head was full of cotton wool and it seemed that she was getting nowhere very fast.

'Rebecca—you need to come with me now.'

He used a commanding tone but, hazy though she might be, she knew that this was one area where she had to stand her ground. 'I'm not going anywhere without Connor. I need you to give me a hand with the stretcher.'

He didn't waste any time arguing with her. Instead, he grabbed hold of the end of the stretcher by Connor's head and she lifted up the other end. Between them they slowly negotiated their way through the cabin towards the exit and Craig began to ease himself through the open door.

'I'll take the weight. Rest the stretcher on the metalwork to take the strain and keep hold of the frame as best you can. The current is fast and strong out here, so you need to be ready for that. Do you think you can manage?'

'Of course.' She sent a swift glance over to where the pilot was sitting. He was wearing a helmet but she could see a trickle of blood seeping from beneath it, running down his face. Beside him, the copilot was clutching his chest and struggling for breath.

'I'll come back for you, Tom,' Craig said reassuringly.

'That's OK. I'm not going to leave Harry.'

Outside, the storm was blowing hard, whisking Rebecca's hair back from her face and tossing the strands in all directions. The sky was a threatening grey, and rain was falling. Craig paused, sliding a canvas cover in place over Connor's head, like a tent.

'Are we ready?'

Rebecca nodded, and slid cautiously down into the water. The river was wide at this point, and she guessed that they must have come aground in a tidal inlet, where the river spilled out into the sea. The shoreline was rugged here, with shelving sands and grassy hillocks, and in the distance low mountains loomed, their summits covered in mist.

She shivered again. Her teeth were chattering, and the water was swirling about her, but at least her feet were on the ground, and she used all her strength to wade against the tide and keep the stretcher above the waves.

When they finally made it to shore, they carefully laid the stretcher down on the heather-clad bank, and she fell to her knees and stopped to pull air into her lungs for a moment or two. The trek through that chill water had taken her breath away and her limbs were stiff and painful.

She looked around for shelter. 'If we can find some-where safe, out of the wind, where we can leave Connor for the moment, I'll come and help you with the others.'

'No, I want you to stay here with him. He needs you.' Craig's voice was clipped, brooking no argument. 'Be-sides, the tide is coming in fast, and you're weak already. You're out of breath. You'll slow me down and I don't want to have to watch out for you as well as the crew.' He placed the kitbag on the ground next to her. 'I brought out as much as I could gather together before we crashed. We should have enough medical supplies to keep us going for a while.'

She stared at him, dumbfounded. He was telling her that she was virtually useless, a frail, helpless woman who would hinder him in his efforts, and despite her discomfort she was mad enough to take umbrage at that. She glared at him, opening her mouth to say something sharp and pithy, but he was already moving back into the water, and Connor was calling to her, his voice thin and reedy.

'Becca, what's happening? Why are we here?' He was struggling to get the words out, and she guessed that the infection in his chest was taking hold.

She turned to the boy, going down on her knees and leaning over him to protect him from the worst of the weather. How was she going to explain to him what had happened? He had already been through one disaster, and he was still suffering from the after-effects from it, so how would he cope with knowing that yet another accident had come about?

'We have to wait here for a while…just until we can sort out another way to get to the hospital.' She wasn't sure how much he understood of what had happened. He had been asleep for the most part, and he was probably a little disorientated. 'The weather was too bad for us to go on any further in the helicopter.'

'My chest is sore,' he said. 'It hurts me to breathe.'

'I'm going to give you another dose of medicine,' she told him. 'It'll be an injection this time…so it should get to work quicker.'

Her fingers were numb with cold, making her struggle with the clasp on the medical bag, but after a while she managed to open it and take out the syringe and medication. Another light sedative might help to take the edge off any worries Connor had, and then she would do what she could to keep him warm and comforted.

She gave him the injection and then looked back over

the stretch of water. The grim outline of the helicopter, tipped on one side, its dark undercarriage broken and twisted, was a grim reminder of how they had dropped from the sky.

Where was Craig? There was no sign of him, just the hulk of the machine against the skyline, and even as she watched it seemed to shift position and lurch even more to one side.

Perhaps if she could sort out the immediate problem of the child's safety, she would be able to go and help with Craig's rescue mission.

'Let's find you a place somewhere out of this wind,' she told Connor. 'There's an overhang of a crag just beyond the shore. That might help to keep us a bit warmer.'

Connor's eyes were already closing again, and she took advantage of his drowsiness to haul the stretcher across the hillocks of earth to where the ground rose into a steep promontory. In the lee of the outcrop of rock, there was a pebble-strewn floor, where she could safely bring the stretcher to rest. Overhead, foliage sprouted from the cliff face, providing temporary cover.

'I'm going back to fetch the bags,' she said. 'I'll be two minutes, that's all.' She didn't know whether or not he heard her. His eyes stayed closed, and in a way that was a blessing. He didn't need to know what was going on.

Out in the estuary, she saw that Craig had emerged from the helicopter and was coming ashore, and a huge sense of relief flooded over her. He looked strong and vigorous, a determined man invincible against the storm. Tom was with him, and both men were supporting the injured pilot. Craig was taking most of the pilot's weight, with Harry's arm draped across his shoulder and the bulk of his body leaning across his back, but Tom was carrying something, keeping whatever it was above the level of the water.

Rebecca hurried over to them and tried to lend a hand as they started to scramble to shore. 'Let me take that from you,' she murmured, relieving Tom of his load. 'Do you want me to take over with Harry? I can take some of the strain from you.'

'We'll manage, thanks.' Tom was struggling, but he kept on walking, and Rebecca glanced at Harry to see what kind of a state he was in.

Rain had washed away the blood from his face, but there was a huge bump on his forehead and his eyes were closed, his feet stumbling across the ground. She guessed that he was concussed, but at least he was alive, and that was the main thing.

'I've put Connor over there, by the promontory,' she said. 'At least we can be out of the main thrust of the wind back there, and that will give us the chance to take a look at your injuries.'

Once they reached the outcrop of rock, Craig eased Harry gently down into a sitting position, where he could support his back against the cliff face. Tom dropped to the ground by the side of him. He was clearly exhausted.

'I want to take another look at you, Harry,' Craig said. 'Can you understand what I'm saying?'

'Yes,' Harry muttered.

'I just need to check your reflexes,' Craig told him, holding out his penlight and shining it into Harry's eyes. 'Follow the direction of the light for me, will you?'

Harry did as he asked. 'I feel sick,' he said.

'That will be the concussion,' Craig murmured. 'I don't think you have any major injuries, but we need to keep an eye on this bump on your head, so I'll need to check your neurological responses every so often. In the meantime, I'll give you something to take the pain and nausea away.'

While Craig was doing that, Rebecca rummaged in her medical bag and came up with a disposable kidney bowl. 'Keep this by you if you think you might be sick,' she told Harry in a sympathetic tone. 'You took a nasty jolt, and it's not surprising that you're feeling pretty awful right now.'

'I'm sorry that I got you into this mess,' Harry mumbled.

'You didn't do anything wrong,' Rebecca said quickly. 'You mustn't think that way. You and Tom saved our lives, and we'll always be grateful to you for that.'

By now Craig was busy examining Tom. 'It looks as though you've cracked a few ribs,' he said, 'but as far as I can tell there isn't any other internal damage. We'll need to confirm that, of course. I'll give you a strong painkiller, but it's best if we don't bind the chest because it could interfere with your breathing and cause more problems.'

'That's all right.' Tom leaned his head back against the rock. 'Just as long as we can rest here for a while.'

Rebecca was checking up on Connor. The child's breathing was fast and he had developed a troublesome cough.

'How is he doing?' Craig asked softly. 'He doesn't look too well.'

'He isn't. I'm worried about him because this has come on very quickly.' Rebecca frowned. 'I'm beginning to think that he must be suffering from a post-operative infection that's been building up for some time, and it's possible that he'll need to have the fluid drained from the pleural cavity before it affects his breathing too badly. The best thing would be to flush the cavity with antibiotic solution, but conditions out here aren't good for that. I just don't know how long we can wait.'

She sent him a quick glance. 'How long do you think it will be before anyone comes looking for us?'

Craig gave it some thought. 'I should imagine they've already set up a search and rescue operation. I doubt they'll be able to get a helicopter out in this weather, but they should manage to launch a lifeboat and land ambulances. It's all a question of knowing where we are, but Harry managed to get out a Mayday call before we came down, and the locator beacon should be working.'

'So we just sit and wait? Hopefully it will be a land ambulance that reaches us first.'

'Why do you say that?' He sent her a quizzical look. 'Because of the medical facilities, you mean? I don't think it matters either way, because I imagine they'll send a doctor and equipment along with the lifeboat.'

'No, it isn't that. It's because I'm a Jonah,' she said miserably, 'and I wouldn't like to be responsible for what happens if we set foot on a lifeboat. I haven't had much luck so far with air transport. I feel as though I'm a disaster waiting to happen.'

His mouth twisted in amusement. 'You're alive. We're all alive. That can't be bad, can it?'

She made a face. 'Maybe that's true, but Connor's ill and this cold air is not doing him any good at all.'

He nodded. 'I know.' He glanced at the package that Tom had been carrying. 'That's why we thought to grab some insulating blankets and a waterproof sheet when we came away from the helicopter. I think perhaps we should try to keep warm by wrapping them around ourselves.'

Rebecca cheered up a little at the news. 'That was good thinking. Are there enough to go around? I want to make sure that Connor is covered up first of all.'

'There should be, but if there aren't, I dare say you and I could always share,' Craig murmured. He said it with a smile and kept his voice low so that the others would not hear, a glimmer lighting his eyes.

Soft colour flushed her cheeks. 'I doubt that will be necessary,' she said. Her grey gaze slanted over him. Didn't anything ever faze him? Here they were in a terrible situation, but it seemed as though he was taking it all in his stride.

She started to open the package that Tom had retrieved from the helicopter, taking out one of the insulated sheets and wrapping it around Connor, ensuring that he was warm, at least.

Craig was shaking out the rest of the sheets, wrapping one first of all around Harry then making sure that Tom was adequately covered with another.

Moving away from the two injured men, he went over to Rebecca and held out a silver foil sheet. 'Your turn,' he said.

He started to fold it around her, and she said lightly, 'I can manage, thanks.'

'OK.' He looked at her oddly, and she wondered if he was taken aback by her need to do this for herself.

She said in a strained tone, 'Do you think we could use the waterproof cover as a windshield?'

'Yes, I imagine so, if I can find a way to rig it up. I'll see what I can do.'

In the end, he bound a corner of the waterproof sheeting around one of the overhanging branches, stringing it up in front of the small group of people until the other end met up with a protruding piece of rock where he could fasten it in place. 'That should hold for a while,' he said.

Rebecca went to seat herself beside Connor. The child was asleep, and she was thankful for that. Harry and Tom looked as though they were shattered by the experience they had been through, and neither of them was speaking. Harry was leaning his head back as though it was all too much for him, and Tom had closed his eyes, trying to grab some rest while he could.

Rebecca shivered, but whether it was from thoughts of what had happened in the last hour or so or from the chill of waiting through the storm she couldn't tell. Her fingers were cold and aching, and her lips were stiff with tension.

The events of the day were beginning to crowd in on her. Most of all she was fearful for Connor's well-being, and she wasn't sure how much longer he could go on without having access to the facilities of a well-equipped, modern hospital.

Craig came and sat beside her. 'Actually, I do think it would be a good idea to huddle together for the sake of keeping warm. Tom and Harry are close enough together to keep the cold from one another, at least. We've no idea how long we are going to have to wait and the last thing we need is for any of us to suffer from hypothermia.'

He slid an arm around her. 'Let me try to warm you.'

He smiled at her. 'I'm being serious now. I just want to keep you from freezing to death.'

She nodded. 'All right.' She cautiously leaned into him, and he folded her against the wall of his chest. She said in a low voice, 'Do you think the rescue services will find us tucked away back here?'

'They will, I'm sure of it.' He held her close, and she snuggled into him, thankful for the shelter he offered her in spite of her niggling doubts about cosying up to someone she had only met a couple of days ago. They had been through so much together already, so perhaps none of that mattered any more.

At least they were both shielding Connor from the wind that blew around the waterproof sheet, and Craig appeared to have enough warmth and strength for both of them. He wrapped both of his arms around her, keeping her tightly pressed against the bulwark of his body.

Slowly, the feeling started to creep back into her limbs, and she began to sense that things might after all turn out all right. Craig's cheek was resting against her forehead, and that simple touch of human warmth spread inside her like a flame, heating her through and through until she began to feel that she was whole once more.

She almost didn't want this closeness to come to an end. She was secure in his arms, safe from the clamour and heartbreak of the world outside, and for these few peaceful moments in time that was all she craved.

CHAPTER FIVE

THAT wonderful feeling of warmth and blissful closeness had somehow disappeared. Rebecca opened her eyes and blinked for a second or two, giving herself time to work out exactly what it was that had changed.

Gazing around her, she saw that she was still sitting in the shelter of the promontory. Tom and Harry were sleeping, or at least their eyes were closed. Connor was coughing, and that alarmed her until she realised that Craig was by the boy's side. He had the medical kit open on the floor, and she noticed that he had laid out various pieces of medical equipment on a sterile sheet.

'What are you doing?' she said. Her voice came out in a husky mumble, and when she tried to move, her limbs were stiff from the cold.

'I'm going to insert a thoracotomy tube into the pleural space so that we can drain away the fluid from his chest. The infection seems to be taking over, and I'm afraid that his lung will be affected if it gets any worse. I want to infiltrate the area with antibiotic solution and afterwards we can carry on with intravenous medication.'

He glanced at her, and she guessed he was trying to

assess the state she was in. 'I didn't want to wake you up because you seemed so peaceful when you were asleep.'

'I wasn't really sleeping, was I? I wanted to stay alert for Connor.' Dismayed, Rebecca looked over at the boy. The child's face was flushed with fever and he looked very ill.

'His coughing must have disturbed you, the same way that it did me. I doubt that you would have left him for long without going to check up on him.'

That was something, at least. She looked at the equipment he had laid out. 'Are you quite sure that this is the place to be doing that? Shouldn't we wait until we can get him to hospital?'

'I don't think we have any choice,' Craig said, his tone blunt. 'If I can get the tube in place, at least it will relieve the pressure and help him to breathe more easily. I'm aiming to keep conditions as sterile as I possibly can.'

'I'll help you,' she said.

'That's not necessary.'

Rebecca frowned. She kneaded her fingers together to try to instill some warmth into them. 'I'll put on some surgical gloves. I'm not sure I could do the procedure myself with my hands being so cold. Are you absolutely sure that you can manage?'

His mouth made a crooked shape. 'Don't worry. I won't do him any harm. I've done this procedure lots of times before, and I've anaesthetised the area, so he shouldn't suffer in any way.'

'I didn't mean that. It's just that I don't know how it is that you're able to rise above the conditions this way, when the rest of us are clearly feeling the effects of cold and shock.'

Was she weak, as he had implied earlier? She had always tried to be independent, and do her best to deal with everything that came across her path, but these last few hours had challenged her more than anything that had come before, and she was having to dig deep into her reserves of strength.

He, on the other hand, had been completely in control of the situation from the start, and nothing had daunted him. She couldn't make him out. Was he really as tough as he appeared to be? Did nothing stop him in his tracks?

Craig was already making the incision between Connor's ribs. She watched him insert the Kelly clamp and then feel for the pleural cavity. He pushed in the chest tube and then removed the clamp, advancing the tube a little further. Once he was satisfied that the tube had entered the cavity, he removed the trocar and clamped the outer end of the tube with the Kelly.

After a minute or so, when he had done everything that was necessary and had sutured and taped the tube in place, Rebecca handed him the suction unit so that he could allow drainage of the infected fluid.

'I gave him an antibiotic injection some time ago. I don't have my watch or my phone to rely on any more, so I'm guessing about the amount of time that has passed,' she said. 'I don't know whether it would be too soon to give him another dose.'

'I don't suppose it has been all that long,' Craig murmured. 'It just feels like it.' He made a wry smile. 'I know what you mean about the watch and the phone—I guess they were ruined when the plane ditched.'

'Even yours?' she asked. When she had looked at his wrist earlier that day, she had noted that he was wearing what had looked like a very expensive, designer watch, but now it appeared to be missing.

'Even mine. It was smashed when we landed, and my phone ended up underwater.'

'I'm sorry. Does that mean you were hurt? Shall I take a look at your wrist?' She started to move closer to him.

He shook his head. 'No, it's fine.' He sent her a glance as though to curb any attempt that she might make to help him, and she cautiously backed off. He obviously didn't want her checking him out. Perhaps he had some misguided idea that any kind of injury would make him less of a man.

'Listen. I can hear something,' Tom said, coming out of his drowsy state. 'Is that a rescue boat? Is it coming our way?'

Craig got to his feet and went to push back the waterproof sheet. He looked out over the horizon. 'I think it probably is. It's some distance away, but it seems to be heading in our direction. I'll go and signal to them, just in case.'

Rebecca stayed with Connor, making sure that he wasn't showing any ill-effects after the procedure. He seemed to be calm enough, and the chest drain was working, so that even without X-rays it looked as though Craig had placed the tube in the correct position.

She got to her feet. 'I'll be back in a minute,' she told the boy, laying a hand lightly on his shoulder.

She went to join Craig, looking out across the water to where a vessel was making swift progress. 'It's the lifeboat, then?' she said.

'It looks that way.'

A quick tide of relief ran through her. 'I'd almost expected an ambulance to arrive here first, but I suppose we're a bit far off the beaten track. There isn't a road nearby, as far as I can see.'

'I expect that's why Harry aimed for this part of the shore as best he could. He would have wanted to minimise any casualties.'

'So what will happen now?'

'They'll probably take us to the nearest port, and there should be an ambulance waiting for us to transport us from there to the hospital.' He sent her an oblique glance, his gaze running over her pale features. 'You don't look too happy about that. I would have thought you'd be ecstatic.'

'I am—at least, I am for all of you.'

'But? There is a but, isn't there?'

Rebecca shifted in discomfort. 'Like I said, I have this horrible feeling that wherever I go, disaster follows. You said lightning didn't strike twice but obviously it did, and all I can think is that I was the one common factor.'

His eyes glimmered with amusement. 'You're not serious? You can't possibly believe that, can you?'

She clamped her lips together, not answering, and he put his arm around her, holding her tightly against him. 'The cold has obviously addled your brain,' he said, giving her a squeeze. 'Don't you realise that you're actually our guardian angel in the flesh? Think what might have happened if you hadn't been there to save us.'

She looked at him, her mouth turning down a little at the corners. He was making fun of her, and she couldn't really blame him, could she? He was right, it must be that the chill air was getting to her.

'Perhaps you've stumbled across your role in life,' he murmured. 'You're here to keep us all from harm.' He looked her over as though he was impressed by what he saw. 'A guardian angel…you know, that is really something special. I can't believe my luck in finding you. I always imagined that my saviour would be an ethereal figure dressed in a white gossamer dress, and here you are with flyaway, windswept hair, all done up in a silver foil blanket. Is that what all the best-dressed angels are wearing these days?'

Rebecca couldn't suppress a chuckle. 'Stop teasing me,' she said. 'It isn't fair.' Besides, she couldn't think straight while he had his arm around her. Her nervous system was already in chaos, and his nearness and his overriding masculinity was playing havoc with her senses.

She looked out over the water once more. 'Perhaps we ought to start getting the equipment together. The sooner we get loaded up, the quicker Connor will be able to receive the treatment he needs in hospital…Tom and Harry, too.'

The lifeboat came to a halt further along the riverbank, and she guessed that the water was deeper back there. Two men disembarked and started towards them, and she saw that they were loaded down with medical bags and equipment.

The first one to reach them checked that everyone was accounted for. 'Is there anyone still in the water?' he asked.

'No, we're all here,' Craig told him, 'but we have some casualties.'

'What exactly are we dealing with?' The second man stepped forward, and Rebecca saw that he was wearing a paramedic's jacket.

'The boy is in a bad way, and the copilot has a few fractured ribs. The pilot has a head injury that needs to be checked out as soon as we get to hospital.' Craig frowned. 'He's not looking too good just now.'

'That's OK. We'll take it from here. Let's get you all safely on board.' The chief lifeboat man started to direct operations, and within minutes Connor was being transported aboard the vessel.

As Craig had pointed out, Harry appeared to be disorientated, and Rebecca winced. That was not a good sign.

'He'll need to have a CT scan as soon as we get to the hospital,' she told the paramedic once they were all on board the lifeboat and on their way. They were seated inside the cabin of the vessel, protected from the harsh wind outside, and the lifeboat was skimming through the water, heading for the mainland. 'And Connor will have to be watched closely for signs of increasing infection.'

'It'll all be taken care of,' the paramedic told her. 'You shouldn't be worrying about any of this, you know. You're a patient yourself until we've had you checked over at the hospital and you get the all-clear.'

'But I'm OK. There's nothing wrong with me.'

'Apart from a mild case of hypothermia and post-traumatic shock,' Craig interjected with a wry smile. 'Do as you're told and sit back and relax for a while. You've had enough excitement for one day.'

She narrowed her gaze on him. 'And I suppose you haven't been through the same ordeal? I don't know how you manage to stay so calm. I don't think I've ever met anybody who had such a jaunty attitude to life. We've just been through a terrible experience, and you look as though none of it has touched you. How is it that you've come to be that way?'

'Of course it has touched me.' Craig stretched his long legs out in front of him. 'I wouldn't be human if I didn't feel that we've had a narrow escape, but I have to look at it from another angle. Bad things happen, but we came through this one and so long as I'm here and I'm fit and healthy, I'll accept that and move on.'

The main paramedic who had introduced himself as Josh handed out cups of hot coffee to Rebecca and Craig. 'Drink these,' he said. 'It'll help to warm you up.'

'Thanks.' Rebecca accepted the drink and sipped cautiously at the hot liquid. 'This is so good.'

Josh smiled. 'We'll soon have you feeling on top form once more.'

She looked up at him. 'Do you know whether Connor's parents have any idea what happened to him? I don't know whether news of the accident has filtered back to anyone except the rescue services.'

'I believe the chief radioed back to Base as soon as we found that you were safe, so if they were worrying, at least they will know that he's unharmed. News of the accident was passed on to the rescue services as soon as the Mayday call came in, and shortly after that it would have gone out on the regional news bulletin. If anyone knew who was on the flight, it's possible that they will be calling in for information.'

'Thanks for that, Josh. At least it's good to know that his parents won't be worrying for too long.'

Josh acknowledged that with a nod, and said, 'I'm going to check up on the others. I take it that you'll both be all right for a while?'

'Yes, we'll be fine. Will you let me know if there are any problems?'

'Of course.'

Tom, Harry and Connor were at the far end of the cabin, being attended to by a nurse, with one of the lifeboat crew acting as an assistant. They were ensuring that the child's condition was being monitored, while Tom and Harry were being given top-up painkilling medication.

Rebecca sent a glance in Craig's direction. 'Is there someone who might be worried about you?' she asked as Josh left them. 'Your parents maybe, or a girlfriend? It can't be good to hear about a helicopter crash through a news bulletin.'

He gave a negligent shrug. 'I doubt that my parents will have any idea that I was on a helicopter coming from Northumberland. Mostly I keep to the Argyll area of Scotland, but this last trip was an out-of-the-ordinary mission to bring a patient in for specialist treatment. My brother is probably too busy working his farm to take much note of what I'm doing in between family visits.'

He swallowed his coffee and then studied her momentarily. 'Would your aunt have been expecting you to arrive home before this?'

Rebecca was thoughtful. 'I don't think so. She knows

that I was making arrangements to come and see her, and I tried to phone earlier to say that I was on my way, but I couldn't reach her. I left a message on the answering machine, but she might have gone out for the day. I know her neighbour takes her out and about sometimes.'

It didn't escape her that he hadn't said anything about a girlfriend waiting for him, but that might be because she was out at work and wouldn't be unduly worried about his whereabouts. There had to be a woman in his life, didn't there? No one could be that masculine and full of energy and be celibate, could they?

'And your parents?'

The question startled her, bringing her back to the present moment. She had been deep in thought just then, and heat filled her at the notion that he might have been able to tell what she had been thinking about. Heaven forbid that he should do that.

She shook her head. 'I don't really see too much of my parents.'

He looked as though he might have been about to ask her more, but one of the lifeboat men came over to them and said, 'We're about ready to dock. A couple of ambulances are waiting at the quayside ready to transfer you to hospital. The paramedics say they'll take the boy in one, and perhaps one of you would like to go with him. The rest of you will be going in the other ambulance.'

'I'll go with him,' Rebecca said quickly. 'He's my responsibility until we get him to the hospital.'

'As you like. I'll pass on the message.'

Within the next few minutes they were escorted off the lifeboat and transferred to the waiting ambulances.

Rebecca sat with Connor, and watched Craig from inside her vehicle as he climbed on board the second ambulance. He turned and looked back at her, mouthing, 'I'll see you at the hospital,' but before she could answer, the paramedic closed the doors on her, and they were whisked away.

'Will I see my mum and dad soon?' Connor stirred and looked at her briefly.

'I think so, Connor.' She smiled at him. 'How are you feeling now?'

'I don't know.' His voice trailed away. 'Yucky.'

'You just need to get some rest. We'll soon have you tucked up in hospital.'

Rebecca watched him, and wondered how much he remembered of what had happened. Hopefully it would all seem like a dream that would soon be forgotten.

When they arrived at the hospital, Rebecca wanted to stay with Connor, but there was a team waiting for him, and as soon as she had recounted the details of his treatment, the nurse prepared to wheel him into one of the side bays.

'His parents are anxious to see him,' she said, and of course that was understandable.

Rebecca said goodbye, adding, 'I'll come and see you as soon as I'm able,' but she couldn't be sure whether he had heard her, because he gave no response and he was already being moved towards the treatment room.

Rebecca watched anxiously as he disappeared from view. He had to get well. The child had been through so much.

'We should take a look at you now and make sure that you're not suffering any ill-effects after that horrendous journey.' Another nurse came to take charge of Rebecca, and for the next half-hour or so she was given a thorough check-up. After she had been given the all-clear, the nurse, Helen, ran a bath for her, and Rebecca luxuriated in the warmth for a while, letting the hot water ease away the strains of the day. She washed her hair and dried it, wrapping herself in a clean hospital gown while she brushed it through until it shone. Then she wondered what she was going to do about her wet clothes.

'It's all right,' the nurse told her. 'I took them into our kitchen and put them through a washing cycle, and they're being tumbled dry at this very minute. Just relax for a while and I'll bring them to you as soon as they're ready. You can go and sit in our day room, if you like. It's comfortable in there, and private. No one else will be using it. I'll take you over there, shall I?'

'Thanks.' Rebecca smiled at the girl. 'I wonder if the men are getting the same kind of treatment? We were all soaked through. Have you heard any news of how they're doing?'

Helen nodded, going to the door of the bathroom and guiding Rebecca along the corridor. 'I've made sure that they'll all have clean, dry clothes to put on when they're ready to leave. Tom's been examined by our emergency registrar, and he'll be all right to go home in a while. His ribs will be sore for a few weeks, but there's no worrying internal damage, so he'll be given a prescription for painkillers. Harry's not so lucky—they're worried that there might be a haematoma forming inside the skull, so it's quite possible that he'll have to go to Theatre for emergency surgery.'

Rebecca's expression was serious. 'I was worried that might happen. I hope he's going to be all right.'

'At least he's in the right place.' The nurse came to a halt just a few yards along the corridor and pushed open a door. 'Here we are. This is our day room. We use it for patients or relatives who need to come and have a few quiet minutes. You shouldn't be disturbed.'

Rebecca glanced around the room. 'It's lovely in here, very bright and cheerful.'

'Yes, it is. There's a coffee-machine, with supplies of milk and sugar,' Helen said. 'Just help yourself.'

'I will. Thanks.' Rebecca smiled, but then became serious once more. 'And Connor? How's he doing? Do you know?'

'We'll admit him to our emergency ward for observation, and then as soon as we think he's ready, he'll be sent back to the surgical ward where he was cared for after his original accident. I think the drainage tube that Craig put in will help to speed up his progress…but, then, Craig's always been a wonderful emergency doctor. I've never known him put a foot wrong.'

Rebecca's eyes widened a fraction. 'You know him?'

Helen smiled. 'Oh, yes. This hospital is his home ground. Didn't you know?'

Rebecca shook her head. 'I didn't.'

'Yes, he's been with our emergency department for a long while. We were all worried when we thought he might have been injured in the crash.'

'I don't know how we would have coped without him,' Rebecca murmured. 'He was a tower of strength, and nothing seemed to throw him. I had the feeling he was planning what he needed to do right from the minute we first realised something was wrong.'

'That's our Craig. You sort of feel instinctively that you can rely on him. I've never known him to let anything get him down, although I would have thought this latest calamity might have shaken him up a bit. You never can tell. He always has that untroubled attitude….or, at least, he has as long as I've known him.'

Helen went back to the door. 'I'll leave you alone in here for a few minutes, then. Just try to relax, take it easy, and I'll be in with your clothes as soon as they're ready. Will you be OK for a while?'

'I will. Thank you.'

Helen left the room and Rebecca went over to the coffee-machine to make herself a drink. She checked that the jug was filled with water and then flicked the switch to heat it up.

It was an odd feeling, being here alone in this hospital room after the trauma of the day. All day long she had been keyed up, living off adrenalin, trying to cope with each event as it happened, and now, all at once, it was over. Everything had been lifted from her, taken out of her hands, and she ought to be feeling so much better by now. Only she wasn't in a good way at all. She was numb inside and, try as she may to come to terms with everything that had gone on, she was finding it incredibly hard.

A few minutes later there was a knock at the door, and she half turned, expecting to see Helen walk into the room. Instead, it was Craig who she saw standing in the doorway.

'Is it all right if I come in?' he asked, and she nodded.

'Of course.'

He looked different somehow, and after a moment she realised it was because he had changed out of his crumpled jeans and was wearing a whole fresh set of clothes, dark trousers that clung his long legs, and a crisp shirt that reflected the blue-grey colour of his eyes.

'You look all spruced up,' she commented lightly. 'I can't believe that the nurse managed to find those in a cupboard somewhere.'

He smiled wryly. 'No. I keep a fresh set in my locker, just in case. You never know when you might need them in this job.'

'I can imagine.' She pulled the gown a little closer around her body. She felt awkward now, half-dressed and still dazed from the events of the day, while he was fresh and alert.

She said softly, 'I was just going to make some coffee. Would you like a cup?'

'I would, thanks.'

She lifted the filter jug and started to pour the hot liquid, but then she stopped suddenly and carefully replaced the glass container on its stand. Her hands were shaking and that was upsetting. She had tried so hard to keep her emotions reined in, but now the strain was proving too much for her. She couldn't even manage this simple task, and it was scary how defencelessness she felt.

'Let me do that for you,' he said. 'You've had a bad day and I would hate to see you scald yourself.'

She nodded and moved away from the worktop, letting him take over. She pressed her lips together. It was frustrating, this inability to take control of the most mundane task, and it was humiliating to have him witness her inadequacy.

'It's just— I'll be fine in a little while,' she managed. 'I think everything must be catching up with me, that's all.' She gave a choked laugh. 'Perhaps I should have gone to bed early last night, instead of partying. That way, I might have been more prepared for the way things turned out.' Her mouth twisted a little. Last night seemed so far away now.

Craig glanced at her, but he continued to pour coffee. When he had finished, she thought he might hand her a cup, and she wondered how she would disguise the fact that she was still feeling shaky. It bothered her a lot. None of this should be happening. She had always been strong, and yet now she was as weak as a kitten.

He left the drinks untouched on the tabletop. 'Come here,' he said in a low, roughened tone. He held out his arms to her, and when she would have hesitated he reached out and drew her into his embrace, holding her close and lowering his head to hers, so that his cheek lightly grazed her face.

'You've been through a hellish day,' he said. 'There's no shame in feeling this way. It's bound to have an effect on you.'

'But it's over now. We're safe, on dry ground, and we haven't been hurt, you and I. I don't understand why I feel as though I'm falling apart.'

'Don't try to understand it,' he said. 'You're human, you do the best you can, and sometimes life takes its toll anyway. You'll feel differently about things in the morning, after you've had a good night's sleep. Don't worry about anything now. It'll pass.'

She looked up at him. 'How do you manage to stay on top of things? How do you keep on going?'

A faint smile touched his mouth. 'I suppose I count my blessings. I'm thankful to be alive. I think about how the one good thing about this day is that it has brought me into contact with a sweet, vulnerable young woman, and it makes me want to take her in my arms and comfort her, just like this…'

His fingers threaded through the silk of her hair, gently caressing the nape of her neck, smoothing away all the tension there. It was such a warm and lovely feeling being held this way, and she found herself wishing that this closeness might go on for ever and ever…or at least, for just a little longer.

She stirred in his arms, lifting her head a fraction, and perhaps that was her undoing because the line of his jaw, already snuggled close to her cheek, shifted with the movement and his lips brushed the softness of her face, sliding down to glide over the tender fullness of her mouth.

A low sigh escaped him, and he lightly tasted the sweetness of her lips.

It was barely a whisper of a touch, not even a kiss, really, but Rebecca's eyes closed, savouring the delicious thrill of that moment. Heat flooded her veins, coursing through every part of her body. She was safe, she was complete, and right now she wanted nothing more than to be held like this, in his arms.

It took a while for sanity to return. Perhaps it was a noise outside in the corridor that made her come back to the raw

reality of the present, or maybe it was that he began to reluctantly ease himself away from her.

In either case, that magical moment drifted to an end and
he looked into her eyes and she began to realise that she
must have slipped into a dream world and lost her senses.

What had she been thinking? Nothing at all, judging
from her reckless actions. Hadn't she learned anything at
all from her bitter experience with Ben? Above all she
ought to have realised that her instincts were sadly misguided where men were concerned.

'Perhaps I should see if I can find Helen and see if my
clothes are ready,' she murmured awkwardly. 'I ought to
go and phone my aunt and start making arrangements to
go home.'

'I'll go and find her for you,' Craig said. His gaze drifted
over her. 'You should stay and drink your coffee. Take a
few minutes more to get yourself together.'

His mouth made a flat line. 'Besides, we both need to
see what we can do about reclaiming some of our lost belongings. I'll do some ringing around for both of us if you
like. I dare say we can make arrangements to replace cash
cards, keys and so on.'

She stared at him. 'I hadn't even thought that far ahead.'

'That's all right. I'll set the wheels in motion. You go
and sit down and drink your coffee. Nothing has to be
done right away.'

He handed her the cup, closing her fingers carefully
around the rim and ensuring that she was steady enough
to be left with it.

'I'll be back in a minute or two.'

She nodded, frowning as she watched him leave the

room a moment later. Did nothing bother him? He was totally in command of himself, and it was as if their moment of closeness had never happened.

Perhaps it was just as well that he was behaving that way. It meant that she, too, could forget about it and move on. Couldn't she?

CHAPTER SIX

'WERE you planning on leaving those French fries?' Craig asked, eyeing up the dish to one side of Rebecca's dinner plate. They were sitting in the hospital restaurant, taking advantage of the mid-afternoon lull in order to grab a bite to eat. Craig had found them a table by the window, overlooking a quiet, landscaped portion of the hospital grounds, and Rebecca was finally beginning to relax.

She speared some tomato and lettuce with her fork, adding a thin slice of red pepper, and then followed the direction of his gaze. 'Yes, I've had enough, thanks. Help yourself.'

He did as she suggested, tipping the lot onto his plate, alongside what was left of his fillet steak and mushrooms. She watched him eat, amazed by the way he managed to tuck away so much food when there wasn't so much as a spare ounce of fat on his torso. 'You must burn it up as soon as you put it away,' she remarked.

He sent her a quick grin. 'Always on the move, that's me. I like to keep busy.'

'I can imagine.'

She felt so much better now that she was dressed in

clean clothes once more, and she had discovered that her jeans and cotton top were none the worse for wear. Helen had brought them to her, along with a cosmetic bag and a few toiletries, and Rebecca had finally realised that she was hungry and ready to get back into the swing of things once more.

'I didn't realise how long it's been since I last ate,' she said. 'The food here is lovely but, then, I suppose you're used to it. I expect you come in here to eat all the time.'

'Mostly, I do, yes. Living on my own, I tend to get my meals wherever I can. Saves me having to cook.'

She smiled across the table at him. 'So do you go home to cadge meals off your parents every now and again?'

He nodded. 'That, too. My mother's not too keen on cooking, but my father's a dab hand in the kitchen. He likes to whisk up exotic meals every now and again, but mostly when I go home it's curry and rice or pizza specials.'

'Specials?'

'Dad's own recipes. You eat it and guess what the herb is that he's tossed in with the tomato purée and assorted meats. My brother's usually the one who works it out, so I'm the one who gets to do the washing-up afterwards.'

She smiled wryly. 'I guess you'll have to take a course in gourmet cuisine if you want to keep your hands dry.'

'Too right.' His mouth slanted. 'Only I don't have had a lot of spare time lately. It seems as though there's always something going on.'

Rebecca finished off her salad and flicked a glance over her dessert. 'I don't suppose you want to polish off the apple pie and custard, do you? I notice you didn't fetch yourself a pudding.'

'I wouldn't dream of taking your sweet from you. Eat it up.' He studied her, a faint line forming between his dark brows. 'You're not on a diet or anything silly like that, are you?'

'Um, no…not really.'

'Good, because you look perfect just as you are. Tuck in and enjoy it. I don't really eat puddings very much. I prefer good, solid food inside me.'

'You're a peasant,' she told him, her mouth curving.

He smiled. 'Very probably.'

Rebecca dipped her spoon into the apple pie. He had said she looked perfect. Did he mean it, or was it simply something that men said to flatter the woman they were with? Still… A tiny glimmer of heat started up inside her.

'So, are you thinking of arranging transport over to the island,' Craig asked, 'or will you wait until tomorrow? Perhaps it would be best to give yourself a break after all that's happened today.'

'My passage over there is already booked,' she told him. 'I think I really want to go and see how Aunt Heather is bearing up. She's such a sweet, lovely woman, and I can't wait to be with her again. She was like a mother to me.'

'Really?' He looked puzzled at that. 'But your parents are still around, aren't they?'

'Yes, they are, that's true, but they don't live locally, or even together, and that's why I haven't told them yet about my decision to come back to Scotland.'

'So they went through a divorce? Or was it just a separation? Do you mind me asking?'

Rebecca shook her head. 'I don't mind. It was a divorce and it happened a long time ago. My father never really stayed properly in touch with my sister and me after that. He was a bit of a wanderer, always looking for something new. My mother went off the rails a bit after they split up, so my aunt took us all in as a temporary measure. Then my mother was taken ill, and the arrangement gradually became permanent.'

'I take it that your mother doesn't live anywhere near your aunt these days?'

'No. She lives with her new husband in Cumbria. I suppose that's not too far away.' She trailed her spoon in the apple. 'I go and visit them from time to time, and we keep in touch by phone.'

'And your sister? You mentioned her a while back, I think. Didn't you tell me that she was supposed to be coming back from overseas?'

'That's right. There was a mix-up over her little girl's passport and they weren't able to travel. I'm not sure quite what's going to happen there, so it looks as though it will be just me and my aunt on our own for a while. I must go and phone to let her know that I'll be on my way.'

'I hope it all works out for you.'

'Thanks.'

They finished off the meal with coffee and mints and then with some reluctance Rebecca pushed back her chair and made ready to leave.

She felt odd about bringing this meal to an end. Was this the last time she would see Craig? Somehow she had become used to having him around, and it made her sad to think that they would be parting company very soon.

Perhaps it was because they had been through so much

together. That must be the reason why she felt so strangely reticent about saying goodbye.

'I want to go and check up on Connor and Harry before I leave,' she told him. 'I heard that Harry was going to Theatre to have the haematoma dealt with, and I want to make sure that he's come through the surgery all right.'

'Me, too. I thought I would hang around until he's out of the recovery room just to be certain that everything is OK.' He sent her a fleeting glance. 'I could go and see what stage they're at, if you like, while you phone your aunt. Then we could perhaps both go and look in on Connor.'

'Yes, that sounds like a good idea.' Instantly, she felt more cheerful. Craig had been so good to her, helping her through the hazards of escaping from the crash and seeing to it that they were all safe and sound and protected from exposure to the elements. He was a good man to have around in a crisis and maybe that was the reason she didn't want to let him go just yet.

Even so, she was wary of this need to go on being with him. Above all, she had to be strong and take care of herself. There was no point in wishing that he might stay around. She had placed her trust in a man before, only to count the cost at a later date.

She gathered up the bag that Helen had given to her, and a minute or so later she left him to go and enquire about Harry while she sought out a payphone and made the call to her aunt.

Instead of her aunt coming to take call, though, there was an answering-machine message, asking her to contact the neighbour. That was very odd, but Rebecca followed the instructions, and in just a few minutes she found that her world was turning upside down all over again.

'When did this happen, Margaret? How bad is it, do you know?' Rebecca was having trouble taking in what her aunt's neighbour was saying to her.

'It was yesterday. She wasn't feeling too well first thing this morning, and then she had a fall, so I decided to take her along to the casualty department to make sure there was no real damage. While we were there, she collapsed. They said that she'd had a stroke, a blood clot on the brain, or so the doctor told me later on.'

Rebecca sucked in a quick breath. 'And is she still in hospital on the island?'

'No, they took her over to the mainland. I think they felt that she might get more specialised attention if she stayed at the hospital there. Apparently there's a unit attached to the main building, where people who've had strokes can receive all the right kind of attention.'

'Are you saying that she's at The Park Vale Hospital?'

'That's right. I don't know how long they will be keeping her there, but I imagine it will be for some weeks at least.' Margaret paused. 'What will you do? Are you going to stay over there? I'm asking because you'll be needing your belongings, won't you? A carrier dropped them off at my house this morning.'

'Oh, I see. Thanks for looking after them for me, Margaret.' Rebecca tried to calm herself by breathing more slowly and deeply. 'This has all come as a bit of a shock to me, and I'm not sure yet what I'll be doing. I'll have to rethink all my plans, but I imagine I will be coming over there to you at some point to collect everything. Would you mind hanging onto the cases until I can get there?'

'Not at all, love. You take your time and work out what you need to do. From what you were telling me earlier, it must be really difficult for you to take all this in, what with one thing and another.'

'Yes, you're right, it is. I'll go and see Aunt Heather right away, if they'll let me. I'll be in touch, Margaret. Thanks for everything that you've done for me and my aunt.'

'You're welcome.'

Craig was waiting for her when Rebecca went up to Connor's ward a few moments later. After all that Craig had done for her, she felt that she needed to go and say goodbye to him and explain what had happened before rushing off to see her aunt.

'Connor seems to be doing a lot better,' he told her, 'and Harry is out of surgery. They think he'll be just fine.'

'That's really good news,' she said.

'Yes, it is.' He sent her a frowning glance, studying her features intently. 'Has there been some problem with your aunt?' he asked. 'I was expecting you to be all fired up and ready to go, but from your preoccupied expression it looks as though there must have been yet another setback.'

Rebecca nodded. 'Sometimes it seems that everything that can go wrong will go wrong.' She pressed her lips together, trying to keep all her pent-up emotions locked in. 'You'd have thought I would be getting used to it by now, wouldn't you? The thing is, my aunt has had a stroke. I don't know how bad it is yet, but she's being looked after here in this hospital—in the stroke wing. I'm going to go over there as soon as I've looked in on Connor. I need to be by her side.' She gave a brief frown. 'It doesn't look as though I'll be going over to the island after all.'

He frowned. 'I'm really sorry about that, Rebecca. Is there anything I can do to help?'

She shook her head. 'You've done enough already, but thanks all the same.' Her teeth lightly grazed her lip as she attempted to think things through. 'I'll have to look into finding myself somewhere to stay here, on the mainland...I suppose I could rent a place for the short term. There's no point in travelling all that way to the island every day when I need to be here, close to my aunt.'

He nodded. 'I can see how this has changed all your plans. It must have come as a huge shock to you.'

'Yes, it has. I just wanted to say thank you for all that you've done for me. I'm going to look in on Connor and then I'm going to go over to the stroke unit. I shan't be able to concentrate on anything until I know how she is.'

He laid a hand on her shoulder, lightly kneading the softness of her flesh with his palm. 'You're not on your own, Rebecca. I'm here if you need me...you know that, don't you?'

She tried a smile. 'Thanks for that.' This wasn't his problem—it was hers, and hers alone, but it was good of him to try to take some of the weight off her. 'I'll go in and say hello to Connor. It's good to hear that he's feeling better.'

Connor's parents were sitting with him in the small side ward. His mother was holding his hand when Rebecca and Craig walked into the room, but she turned and sent them a small nod in greeting as they introduced themselves.

'The nurse told me that you both looked after him on

the journey.' She glanced at Craig. 'She said it was your treatment that helped him on the road to recovery.'

'I wasn't alone in taking care of him,' Craig told her. 'Dr McIntyre started his antibiotic treatment and made sure that he was comfortable.'

Rebecca was standing by Connor's bedside. 'They tell me that you're feeling a bit better,' she said softly. 'Is that right?'

'Yes. It doesn't hurt so much to breathe now.' Connor hesitated. 'I'm still not hungry, though. The nurses keep asking if I want to eat anything, but I don't. They won't give me porridge again, will they?'

She laughed. It was good to hear him talking again. 'Not if you don't want it,' she said. 'I'll have a word with them about it, if you like.'

He nodded and smiled contentedly. 'Crisps,' he said. 'I like crisps.'

'Then we'll have to see what we can do about that,' she murmured. 'I'm sure they'll be able to rustle some up for you.'

She left the room just a little while later, with Craig walking by her side along the corridor. 'I'll go straight over to the unit now, to see my aunt,' she said, sending him a quick glance.

'OK,' he said. 'I hope she's not too poorly. At least you'll know that she's in good hands. The people who run the stroke unit do a really good job.'

'That's good to hear.' She hesitated for a moment, and then said, 'Thanks again for everything that you've done to help me in these last few days, and especially for the way you held everything together today. I'm sure it was your

clear thinking that made sure we all managed to get clear
of the helicopter.'

He smiled at her and took her hand in his, holding it
lightly between his two palms. 'I'm glad that you're safe.'

There was so much comfort to be had from the touch
of his hands, but above all it was distracting, swamping her
with confusion and errant thoughts of what might have
been.

She didn't want to prolong the goodbye. She would
probably never see him again, and somehow that was too
painful to contemplate so she nodded lightly and slowly
began to turn away from him.

He released her and she walked away. How was it that
in such a very short time he had managed to work his way
into her heart?

CHAPTER SEVEN

'I so wanted to be there for you…at home.' Heather said slowly. She was struggling to get the words out, slurring her speech a little, and it was difficult at times for Rebecca to understand what her aunt was saying. It saddened her to see her looking so pale and tired in the hospital bed, her faded brown hair splayed out in wisps over the pillow.

'You don't need to be worrying about that,' Rebecca said. 'I just want you to get well, Auntie. I only wish I'd been here for you when you needed me.'

It was distressing to see her usually energetic aunt struggling to lift her arm and unable to walk. The only positive aspect was that she was still able to speak at all, albeit in a slower, more laboured fashion than usual, and she seemed to be able to understand what Rebecca was saying to her, which was a bonus.

Rebecca glanced over her aunt's hospital chart to satisfy herself that everything possible was being done to make her well again. 'They're giving you medicine to dissolve the clot that's causing the trouble,' she told Heather, 'and along with that they're trying to bring down your blood pressure.' She gave her a smile. 'That means no excitement for the next few weeks.'

'Chance would be a fine thing,' her aunt managed haltingly. She lay back wearily. 'You must take the key to the house.' She tried to signal, indicating her leather handbag, which rested on the bedside locker. 'Make it your own while I'm stuck in here.'

Rebecca shook her head. 'I'm not going over to the island, not while you're in here. I'll make some other arrangements so that I can stay close to you.' She frowned. 'Mind you, I'll have to go back to pick up my belongings at some point. Margaret says she's looking after them for me.' She smiled gently as she patted her aunt's hand. 'It was really good of her to take care of you the way she did. I'll always be grateful to her for that.'

'Aye. She's a fine friend.' Her aunt's brow furrowed. 'You were looking forward to going back to your old home, weren't you?' She managed to indicate that by a series of half-formed words and by using her good arm to make hand gestures and arm movements.

'This is like playing charades,' Rebecca said with a smile. 'Is it a book…is it film? Do you remember how we used to play that game at Christmas and at birthday parties? You were always good at that.'

Rebecca desperately wanted to cheer her aunt up. Heather had always had a good sense of humour and she hoped that she would pick up on the fact that things might not be as bad as they seemed right now.

'Yes, I was looking forward to being back on the island,' Rebecca went on, 'but none of that really matters now. It was you I wanted to see most of all, and at least I'm here with you now. The important thing is that we help you to get back on your feet. I expect they'll start doing physio-therapy and speech therapy with you as soon as you're up to it.'

A nurse came into the room just then with a tray of food for her aunt, and Rebecca stayed to help Heather manage the cutlery.

It occurred to her that if they were serving the patients' evening meals then time was running on, and she still had the task of finding herself somewhere to stay for the night.

'I'll have to go,' she said some time later in a resigned tone, 'but I'll be back here tomorrow to see you. You take care, and try to get some rest, Auntie. At least I know the doctors and nurses will look after you very well, so that makes me feel a little better about leaving you.'

A few minutes later Rebecca dropped a kiss on her aunt's cheek and then she went quietly out of the room, leaving her aunt to doze in the hospital bed.

Her mind was busy with all kinds of thoughts as she hurried along the hospital corridor. Perhaps the first thing she ought to do was to look through the telephone book and pick out a hotel where she could stay for the night. It was too late now to find rented accommodation. All the agencies would be closing up.

'Hey, slow down. I'll walk with you.'

Rebecca's eyes widened as she saw Craig coming towards her. Whereas she was beginning to wilt after the strain of the day, he looked tall and strong and as energetic as ever, and the sight of him gave her senses a lift.

'You're still here,' she said unnecessarily. 'I thought you would have gone home ages ago.'

'I might have done that, but it occurred to me that you might be feeling a bit disorientated and out of synch, having to stay on in a strange place, so I hung about for a bit. I went and checked up on Tom while you were with your aunt.'

He was saying that he had been thinking about her... Why did that come as a surprise after the way he had looked out for her today? He had not for one second let any of them down. She said quietly, 'Is Tom OK?'

'He's doing all right.' He slanted her a sideways glance. 'How did it go with your aunt?'

'I suppose it wasn't too bad...at least, it wasn't as wretched as it might have been. She still has some speech, but she's lost the use of her arm and leg to a large extent. It's a question of giving her the right medication and allowing time for her to heal. Of course, she'll need a lot of physiotherapy in order to regain the function of her limbs.'

It was a sad situation, but even so she gave a faint smile. 'I'm just glad that I was able to be with her at last. I love her to bits and I can't bear to think of her being ill in hospital and separated from her family, so it means that all my plans are out of the window. I need to stay close to her, so I guess that's my next job—finding somewhere to stay.'

He considered that for a moment or two. 'I thought you might have difficulty sorting things out, and it occurred to me that you might be in need of some help. That's partly why I stayed on here.'

A small glow started up inside her. 'That was thoughtful of you—it's too late for me to look at rental properties, so I was going to ring around and see if I could find a hotel, somewhere close to the hospital, preferably. I suppose, if you work here, you must have some idea of where I might find something suitable in the area.'

He nodded. 'As a matter of fact, I know just the place, and it isn't too far away from here—just a ten-minute drive or a short bus ride. I have my car here at the hospital, so I could show you, if you like.'

'That would be good.' She made a wry face. 'I wonder if they would mind me turning up with no luggage, just the clothes I'm wearing and the credit card that the bank organised for me?' She remembered how she had looked askance at Craig when he had turned up with just a holdall at the flat, back in Northumberland. It just went to show that you couldn't judge by appearances alone.

'Actually,' he said in a low tone, 'that wouldn't really matter at all. I wasn't going to show you to a hotel. It just so happens that I have a small house not far from here, and there's a guest room that you're welcome to use.'

Her eyes widened. 'Your place?'

He nodded. 'It's been a really long day for you—for both of us, in fact. It would probably be a lot easier for you to just stay over at my house for a while. The fridge is stocked up and there are plenty of ready meals in the freezer, so at least you won't starve, and it won't cost you anything.'

The suggestion had come out of the blue, and Rebecca wasn't quite certain how to react. She wanted above all to be independent and manage for herself any problems that came along, but this had been a particularly awful day and she wasn't sure she could take any more hassle. Craig's suggestion was more than tempting. 'Are you quite sure about this?'

'Of course.' He sent her a quick grin. 'You weren't planning on throwing any wild parties or anything like that, were you? Not that I mind people enjoying themselves, you understand…it's just that my place isn't all that big and I'd need a bit of notice to get things organised.'

'You're never going to let me live that down, are you?' Rebecca murmured.

'Probably not.'

'All the same, I think I would like to take you up on that offer,' she said softly. 'It's getting late, and I wasn't looking forward to searching around for a place. It'll just be a temporary arrangement, of course. I'll look for somewhere as soon as I'm back on my feet—tomorrow.'

'There's no rush. You can take all the time you need. I'm not going anywhere, and I just rattle around in the place on my own.' He sent her a searching glance. 'Are you ready to go? I'll take you there now.'

He had been right when he'd said it was just a few minutes' drive away, she discovered, but none of what he had said prepared her for the sight that met her eyes.

He had said that the place was small, but there was nothing small about it. The house was set in its own grounds, backed by low hills and woodland so that it was immediately pleasing on the eye. There was a low single-storey block to one side with a beautiful wide entrance porch enhanced by a profusion of clematis that scrambled over the trellis-covered walls. Tacked onto this building was a two-storey element with large double windows, and in front of all of this was a generous paved area, which led onto immaculate lawns with shrubbery to either side.

'I thought you said your house wasn't very big,' she

murmured, her eyes growing large as she took it all in. 'This is fantastic. It's lovely.'

'I'm glad you like it,' he said with a twist to his mouth. 'I suppose size is relative, depending how many people who want to cram in. Compared with my parents' home, this is a bit like a holiday chalet.'

'You were obviously born with the proverbial silver spoon in your mouth if you think this is just a holiday home,' she told him. 'A lot of people would give their eye teeth for somewhere like this.'

'I suppose I'm fortunate,' he agreed. 'I was looking for a place of my own when I came to work at the emergency department and for a while it looked as though I wasn't going to find anything that suited me. I wanted somewhere that was close to the hospital, but at the same time in a kind of rural setting. Then this place came on the market and I snatched it up. I like the woodland setting, and at the back of the house, from one of the bedrooms, you can look out over the river in the distance. It can be quite beautiful in the summer, or even in the late autumn.'

'I can imagine.'

'Let's go inside, anyway. I should think you want to wind down. I'll make us some supper and show you the guest room.' He was opening the front door as he spoke and then he ushered her inside.

The interior of the building was every bit as wonderful as the outside. The floor was pale oak, and all the wood-work reflected the same warm colouring. Everywhere was light and open, allowing the last rays of the evening sun-light to filter into every crevice.

'I'll put the kettle on, and then I'll give you a quick tour, if you like. Come through to the kitchen with me.'

She followed him and halted in the doorway of the large room. It was a dream kitchen, with cream-coloured cupboard units and smooth marble worktops. In the centre of the room was a glass dining table, with dancing light shimmering on its surface.

He flicked the switch on the kettle, and said, 'Let me show you the living room. It's just through here.'

He led the way, opening the door to a spacious, rectangular room, furnished with comfy sofas upholstered in a soft cream fabric and decorated with scatter cushions. At the far end of the room was a dining unit with a circular, light oak table and chairs facing patio doors that looked out over a landscaped garden and fields beyond.

'This is all so lovely,' she told him. 'The view out there reminds me of my aunt's cottage on the island. I spent most of the last years of my childhood playing in the fields, gathering wild flowers and feeding the horses that grazed around there. There was a brook where my sister and I used to dangle our nets and try to catch tiddlers.'

'It sounds as though you had fun.'

She nodded and smiled, reminiscing. 'They were happy times when my aunt and uncle took us in. It gave my mother a breathing space to get her head right after everything that had happened, with the divorce and so on, and as far as my aunt was concerned, I think she was glad that we were there with her after my uncle died. We were a comfort to her.'

'Did your mother stay there with you for a long time? You said that she was ill, and I had the impression that she might not have been with you the whole time. You've spoken more about your aunt than you have about your mother.'

He was obviously far more astute then she had counted on. 'I suppose the truth of the matter is that my mother was there with us in body if not in soul,' she said. 'Of course, it's true that she was ill for a while. I think she was run down after everything that had happened with my father, and stress took its toll on her for a while. Once she had recovered, though, I think she became restless. We, Alison and I, tended to turn to Aunt Heather for comfort and companionship. She was always ready to listen to us, and nothing was too much trouble for her.'

She smiled, remembering those days. 'She would walk with us along the country lanes, and she would point out all the things that we might have missed—the wild flowers, the fungi around the roots of the trees, and she was always the one who would spot the squirrel trying to hide from us, or the pheasant that would appear from under a hedgerow.'

'I think I'd quite like to meet your aunt,' he said softly. 'She sounds like a woman after my own heart.'

'I'm sure you would take to her,' Rebecca murmured.

Craig nodded and started towards the kitchen once more. 'I'll make a pot of tea, and then, while it's brewing, I'll show you the rest of the house. There are three bedrooms upstairs, two of them looking out over the fields and the woodland, so if you think you might like to look out over the river, you could have the room next to mine. The other bedroom is smaller, but there's still a good aspect over the front of the house. I'll leave it to you to decide which one you want.'

Rebecca wasn't at all sure about sleeping in the room next to his. Somehow that seemed altogether too close. He wasn't pushing the issue, though, and perhaps she was too much on edge and not thinking clearly. The truth was, she was far too aware of him. He was the first man in a long time who had made her feel that it would be good to have him around.

She followed him up the stairs a short time later and peeped into the master bedroom when he pushed open the door. Somehow, the thought of him sleeping in there made her feel warm all over. She was glad when he pulled the door closed and showed her into the bedroom next door.

'Oh, this is so pretty.' She turned to look at him. 'There's such a contrast between this and…and your room. Does this room belong to someone?'

He shook his head. 'My brother and his wife stay here from time to time. I think Jenny is glad of a break from the farm sometimes so she kind of revels in the chance to chill out around the place. She helped to choose some of the interior decoration. I have my own tastes, but she was good at adding those touches that make a place a home, so I gave her free rein in here. My brother's like me—he doesn't really have any particular preferences, so he lets her get on with it.'

Rebecca laughed. 'Now, he sounds like a man that I would get along with very well.'

He made a smile. 'Actually, you might be better off in this room because, now I come to think of it, my mother bought some packs of underwear and a few items of clothing, just in case anyone was to stay over and didn't have everything that they might need.'

He made a face. 'I think, to be honest, she wasn't just thinking of Jenny—she was thinking that she might forget to pack something or other whenever she came over here. She does that, my mother... She decides to drop by for a weekend and then realises she's forgotten half of the stuff that she needs. My father went away with her on holiday once and found that she'd failed to pack any trousers for him, so now he always does his own packing.'

Rebecca chuckled. 'I can imagine.'

'Anyway,' he added, 'this way, there's no problem. So what I'm trying to say is you could help yourself to any of the things in the wardrobe or the drawers. At least that would tide you over until you get your luggage back.'

She nodded. 'That sounds like a good idea—if you're sure that no one will mind me using any of the clothes?'

'There's absolutely no problem. Just help yourself.' He moved further into the room and pushed open another door. 'You have your own en suite in here, so hopefully you'll have everything you need.'

'Thanks.' She looked up at him, taking in his strong-boned features, the straight nose and the way his mouth was perfectly moulded. 'You're being very good to me. I do appreciate it.'

'Any time,' he said. 'Why don't I leave you here to rummage around for a bit, while I go and rustle up some supper for us?'

'That would be good, thank you.'

It was only when he had left her alone and gone downstairs that she realised she had agreed to sleep in the room right next to his. She glanced towards the large bed with its exquisite soft duvet. The headboard was set against the adjoining wall, and if she remembered right, his bed was just on the other side of that wall.

She gave a soft sigh. How was it that she managed to get herself into these situations? It looked as though she was in for a sleepless night.

CHAPTER EIGHT

THERE was a knock on the door, and then Rebecca heard Craig's voice coming to her from the landing outside the bedroom. 'I'll be putting breakfast on the table in about half an hour,' he said. 'Is that all right with you? I thought I heard you moving around in there.'

'Yes...yes, that will be fine. Thank you.' Rebecca frowned. She had been as quiet as a mouse, hadn't she, so how had he managed to hear her? He must have been on the alert the whole time.

She'd had it in mind to go downstairs and cook breakfast for him, if only as a small way of thanking him for putting her up for the night, but that was out of the question now, wasn't it?

Of course, she hadn't bargained on sleeping from the moment her head had touched the pillow until just a few minutes ago. The events of the previous day must have knocked her for six, because even though her senses were heightened to an abnormal degree where Craig was concerned, and she had been cautious about letting her guard down for even a moment, she had gone out like a light once she'd pulled the duvet protectively around her.

Quickly, she wriggled into her jeans. Then she unhooked a cotton top from its hanger in the wardrobe and pulled it down over her head. It fitted snugly. She followed up with a few quick strokes of the brush through her long hair, and then added a light touch of make-up to her face.

Feeling a little more ready to face the world, and Craig in particular, she went downstairs to the kitchen a few minutes later. The appetising smell of bacon and eggs wafted over to her.

'Good. There you are,' Craig said with a smile, turning as she walked into the room. 'You're just in time.' He slid a plate full of food onto the table and indicated a chair. 'Sit down and tuck in.'

'I feel bad about this,' she said awkwardly. 'About you cooking for me and waiting on me, I mean. I meant to get up early and do all this for you.'

'There's no need for you to do anything at all.' He stood for a moment, simply looking her over from head to toe. 'Just having you here in my kitchen, looking totally gorgeous, is reward enough.'

Her mouth made an odd shape in response to that, something halfway between a smile and a nervous twist. 'You have a smooth tongue in your head, don't you?' she murmured. 'Perhaps I should tell you that I'm very cautious about men like you. I've had my fingers burned before this and I'm not likely to fall for flattery.' She glanced at the table, laid out with toast and butter, apricot preserve and a steaming pot of coffee. 'There's always the chance that bacon and eggs might do it, of course. I do appreciate a good breakfast.'

He chuckled. 'Then you should sit down and enjoy it. I

like a woman with a good appetite.' He started to pour coffee for both of them. 'Incidentally,' he said in a matter-of-fact tone, 'it wasn't intended as flattery. I meant every word of it.' He slid into a chair and reached for a slice of toast. 'I have to say that you're the best-looking woman to come my way in a long, long time.'

She shook her head. He was irrepressible, wasn't he? She said lightly, 'I'm not even going to go there.' Picking up her fork, she started to make inroads on her breakfast. 'Do you have plans for the day?' she asked after a while. 'I suppose under normal circumstances you would be working, wouldn't you?'

'That's right, but I've been told that I have to take a day or so off work to get over the accident. The powers that be aren't letting me have any choice in the matter.'

She frowned. 'Would you have gone in otherwise? I would have thought you would be hesitant after what happened, especially as you are quite often involved in call outs…how can you face going up in a helicopter ever again?'

He shrugged. 'I want to work, and I don't have a problem with the job that I do. Anyway, I think it's probably best to get back on the horse right after you've been thrown, so to speak.'

She stared at him and gave a small shudder. How could he be so casual about what had happened to them? 'Some people might say that would be tempting fate. I certainly won't be setting foot in a helicopter ever again, that's for sure.'

He glanced at her. 'I think that would be a mistake. You can't go through life being afraid of what might happen.'

'You're welcome to think that way. Personally, I don't know how you can go on doing that kind of work after what we went through.'

'The simple answer to that is that someone has to do it. Sometimes it's the only way to make sure that people get to hospital in the shortest time possible after an accident. At least in this line of work I'm able to feel that I'm doing some good.'

She winced. 'I'm sure you are, but if it was me, I'd say that was the end of my time spent up in the air in a tin box.'

'I've never really thought of it that way.' He munched thoughtfully on a corner of the toast that he had dipped into the runny yolk of his egg. 'What about your plans? You had it in mind to go and work on the island where your aunt lives, didn't you? There was a job waiting for you. Isn't that the reason you came here?'

'Yes, I do have something lined up, but I'm not sure how it will work out yet.'

'It involves working with mothers and babies, doesn't it? I heard something about that from one of the nurses. I think you must have told her something about your reasons for coming home.'

She nodded. 'That's right. I'm desperate to get back to my roots. I want to go and live on the island where I grew up. It's the one place where I knew peace, and I long to be there once again. Here on the mainland, where we used to live, my parents were always arguing with each other, and we were under the constant threat of having our family split apart at any moment. It wasn't a good time.'

'So the idea of going back to the island is for you to live and work there on a permanent basis?'

'Yes, that's right.' She sent him a quick glance. 'You sound as though you think that's not a good idea?'

He shrugged. 'I prefer to live and work on the mainland. At the moment I have the best of both worlds, because I work in the A and E unit most of the time and go out with the helicopter on a rota basis. It suits me to do that.'

'Don't you have any qualms at all about going back up in the air?'

He shook his head. 'Like I said, sometimes you have to go with the flow and take the knocks, or life will grind you down. I prefer to put all that behind me and look to the future. I can't govern what happens, so I'll carry on doing what I know best.' He ran his gaze over her. 'Are you going to follow up on the island job? I would have thought that could be a problem if you want to be near to your aunt.'

'That's true, it would.' Rebecca took a moment to savour the taste of fried tomatoes before adding, 'Anyway, nothing is written in stone at the moment. I'm not altogether sure that the job I've been offered will actually come about, but there's always the option of a post in the health centre over there, dealing with the under-fives and their health problems. Again, the centre is waiting for a staff member to finish her contract with them before she moves on.'

'So that leaves you in a kind of limbo right now?'

'Yes, it does.' She frowned. 'For the moment I need to find some other kind of work to tide me over so that I can stay close to my aunt while she's in the stroke unit.'

Craig was thoughtful for a while. 'I could probably help out with that. I imagine I might be able to find you some temporary work in A and E over here. We're always short-staffed.'

'You could?'

He nodded. 'I take it that you've had a fair amount of experience with emergency medicine?'

'Yes, I have…but there's no way I would be prepared to go out on your kind of missions.' She sent him an anxious glance. 'Would I need to do that?'

'Not unless you wanted to.' He studied her briefly before finishing off his meal. 'Would you like me to put in a word for you?'

'That would be great, thanks.'

'Good. That's settled, then.' He appeared to be running it over in his mind. 'I could mention it to Admin this morning when I go to the hospital…I'm assuming that you want to go over there to visit with your aunt for a while?'

'Yes, I do. I thought I would take a bus over there straight after breakfast.'

'There's no need for that. I'll drive you in. I have one or two loose ends that I need to tie up back at the hospital.'

'Thanks.' Rebecca smiled at him before swallowing down the rest of her coffee. Things seemed to be working out far better than she had expected, and it was mostly down to Craig. How was it that her life had been a complete mess up until now, and yet within days of meeting him her path was being smoothed out for her?

A sudden thought brought her up sharply. At this rate she was going to find herself relying on him, and that would never do, would it? He was just someone she had met by chance, and surely in the end they would simply be ships that passed in the night?

'And I imagine there are probably a few things that you need to deal with here on the mainland if you're going to be staying a while.' Craig got to his feet and started to clear away the empty plates.

'Like bringing my suitcases over here,' she murmured. 'Yes, you're right. I'll have to get things organised.'

'Would you like me to take you over to the island so that you can retrieve your belongings? I can imagine that you don't want to fly over there, but I could take the car and drive it onto the ferry, so there shouldn't be any problem… It's just that going over there that way will take up most of the day. We wouldn't be home until late evening.'

'Getting back late doesn't bother me, but are you sure about taking me there? Would you mind doing that for me?' Rebecca pushed back her chair and went to help him with the crockery. It seemed like a lot to ask of him.

'Not at all, but we need to keep an eye on the time we're to catch the lunchtime ferry. At least we've made an early start with breakfast.' He began to stack plates in the dishwasher. 'Besides, the weather is beautiful today, and the view of the islands from the deck of the ferry is quite spectacular, so it would be a break in itself. And we could always get a meal or a drink on board.' He smiled, thinking about it. 'I quite like the idea of spending an hour or so exploring Islay. We could take time out to wander along the shoreline. I think it would do you good to have some downtime.' He threw her a quick glance. 'How does that sound to you?'

Rebecca stared at him, her eyes widening. For the first time in a long while she felt a slow wash of happiness ripple through her. 'I think…' The breath snagged in her throat and she tried again. 'I think that sounds wonderful.'

He pushed the door of the cabinet closed and turned away from the dishwasher to face her. 'Good,' he said.

He moved towards her just as she stepped forward, and in that instant they were so close to one another that it seemed altogether a natural gesture for her to lightly rest her palm on his upper arm.

'You've been such a strong support to me, right from the first,' she said softly, looking up into his blue-grey eyes. 'And now you're being so good to me, all over again, helping me out this way…letting me stay here and offering to take me over to Islay. I'm so grateful to you. I don't know how I would have managed without you.'

'I'm sure you'd have done very well for yourself, left to your own devices.' His mouth softened and he reached for her, returning the simple embrace with a gentle hug, his arms folding around her and bringing her close into the shelter of his body. 'I can't help thinking about how brave you've been. I had to admire the way you clung onto Connor's stretcher when we were about to ditch. You were determined not to let go of him, and afterwards I could tell that his well-being was the first thought that crossed your mind.'

He smiled down into her eyes. 'You would have coped under any circumstances. You were prepared for any eventuality, and you were determined to succeed. Those are two great qualities to be blessed with when you're faced with a crisis.'

'Maybe.' She was finding it increasingly difficult to concentrate on what he was saying. His hands were making slow, sweeping movements along the length of her spine, setting up a spiral of tingling sensation to run throughout the whole of her body, and somehow he seemed to sense that.

He drew her against him, so that the softness of her breasts was crushed against the hard wall of his chest, and that was her undoing. It felt so good to have him hold her this way that she lost all thought of time and place, giving herself up to the tender rapture of being in his arms.

He bent his head towards her, and even as she wondered if this was a kind of madness that had overtaken her and that maybe she should think before throwing caution to the wind, his mouth claimed hers in a whisper of sensation. Her lips softly parted beneath his and she gave a tremulous sigh, giving herself up to the joy of that gentle kiss.

She sensed the quickening of exhilaration within him, too. She felt the thud of his heartbeat against her breast and heard the soft rasp of his breathing as it caught in his lungs. His hands stroked her, lightly tracing the line of her hips and sliding around to linger for a while in the curve in the small of her back.

This was madness, though, wasn't it? The thought spiralled through the haze of excitement that clouded her mind, and the tiny niggle of doubt caused her to ease back from him a fraction. Why was she allowing her emotions to run out of control? Hadn't she learned that relationships were a minefield of trouble and she had to be crazy to even think about going on with this?

His kisses were intoxicating, though. They plunged her into a heady whirlwind of desire and made her want to taste forbidden fruit…

But that was where all her problems would start, wasn't it? She had made up her mind never to trust a man again…not until she had known him long enough to reassure her that he would never do her any harm… And how long had she known Craig?

Five minutes, that was all.

'Becky?' The word came out as a ragged sigh, his breath warm against her cheek, but he must have sensed her withdrawal from him and slowly he let her go.

'That was my fault,' she said. 'I wasn't thinking clearly. I…I didn't mean any of this to happen. I just wanted to let you know that I really am thankful for all that you've done for me.'

'I know that, and it's OK.' He looked at her guardedly. 'Anyway, I should have known better. I don't know what came over me. It's just that you were so close to me and you looked so vulnerable, so much in need of a hug.' He shook his head as though to clear it. 'I should never have done that. You've been through a lot and this is the last thing you need right now.'

He straightened his shoulders. 'Let's get you over to the hospital,' he murmured. 'You could visit your aunt while I go and talk to Admin about the job.'

'Yes, all right.' Rebecca's lips flattened momentarily. She broke away from him and went to gather her things together. It was just as well that they were getting ready to leave, wasn't it? She needed time and space to allow her head to clear. Her nervous system was already shot, and it was doing her no good at all, dallying with a man as compelling as Craig.

'Actually, I think Heather would probably like to meet you,' she said. 'The nurses told her what had gone on with the trip here, and I gather she's curious about you.'

'That's all right. I'll pop my head round the door and say hello.'

* * *

Heather was sitting in a chair by the bed in a side ward when Rebecca arrived at the hospital and went in to see her. Craig introduced himself and brought a smile to her eyes when he inspected her lunch menu. '"Home-made steak pie with a selection of fresh vegetables",' he read aloud. 'Whatever will it be next—caviar and toast? I think I'll have to come and join you.'

He talked with Heather for a few minutes before excusing himself. 'I have to go and see a man about a job,' he said. 'I'll drop by and see you again, if I may?'

Heather nodded, a hint of colour running along her cheekbones. 'I like him,' she said, when he had left the room.

'Yes, he has that effect on people,' Rebecca said in a rueful tone. 'For myself, I'm trying not to get hooked. I've been down that path before.'

She looked her aunt over. 'How are you getting on?' she asked. 'Is there anything that you need?'

'Only to be able to get out of here and go back home,' Heather said haltingly. She managed to add in a painstakingly slow way, 'They say it will be a while before I'm up and about.'

Rebecca nodded. 'I imagine you'll need physiotherapy to help you along a bit.'

'They're going to start it as soon as I'm feeling more up to it.'

'You'll probably start to feel a little stronger every day,' Rebecca said. 'I bought you a newspaper, but I expect you'll have some trouble reading the print, won't you? I wasn't sure how much your vision had been affected.'

'It's not too good. I can't watch the television very well, but the nurse has sorted out the radio for me.'

'That's great.' Rebecca held her aunt's hand in hers, and said quietly, 'I'll see what I can do about getting you some taped copies of the newspaper. I know how you like to keep up to date.'

She stayed with her aunt for a while, until the nurse came to say that the doctor was doing ward rounds and would be along in a few minutes. 'After that,' the nurse told Heather, 'the speech therapist is coming in to see you, to see if we can get you talking again properly.' She smiled. 'Then later on there'll be physiotherapy each day. I hope you didn't think you would be able to lie back and take it easy. People think they come into hospital to have a rest, but sometimes it's busy, busy, busy.'

Heather nodded. 'I guessed as much.'

'I'll come back and see you later this evening,' Rebecca told her aunt. 'I'm going over to Islay to get my cases, so it will take me a while. I'll call in and sit with you tomorrow.'

'OK.'

'And I spoke to Alison on the phone, and she said that she'll give you a ring later on today. She sends her love.' Rebecca gave her aunt a hug and kissed her cheek. 'Try to stay cheerful,' she said. 'You've always been my strength, and Alison's, and we're going to be yours now. We'll see you through this.'

'Bless you.'

Rebecca came away from the room feeling that it was going to be some time before her aunt was back on her feet again. If by any chance Craig managed to find her a job at the hospital, it would be a godsend, because then at least she would be here, on the premises, and able to drop by and see Heather every day.

Craig met her out in the corridor. 'How is she?' he asked with a faint frown. 'She seemed to be in reasonably good spirits earlier.'

'She's bearing up. But, then, she's my aunt and she always tries to make the best of things. That's her way. I think it was a partial stroke, and it could have been a lot worse. This has knocked her back a lot, though.'

She glanced at the clock on the wall. 'Do you think we have time to go and see Connor before we go?'

He nodded. 'Yes, of course. It's still relatively early, but we need to leave here in a few minutes if we're to catch the ferry on time.'

Connor was doing very well, she saw, when they found him a few minutes later. His eyes were bright, and straight away Rebecca could see that he was on the mend.

'The nurses say I might be able to get out of here soon,' he said on a bright note. 'Only, they're going to try letting me go out on trips every few days first, to see how I get on.'

His mother was in the room with him, sitting by his bedside. She gave a quick frown, brushing her dark hair back from her brow in a worried fashion. 'He's been badgering them non-stop ever since he started to feel better. The only trouble is, his father and I are going to be in hospital for a bit longer, so we can't let him go home until we can look after him ourselves. His grandparents are around but they're both getting on a bit, and it seems unfair to put the worry of his care on them.' She looked over at

Connor, her expression serious. 'The thing is, he's desperate to get out of here.'

'That's understandable,' Craig said. 'He's young, and even though he's been very ill, he's getting his energy and strength back.' He was thoughtful for a moment, and then he said, 'I suppose there is a way around the situation, but it depends how you feel about it.'

Connor's mother gave him an enquiring look. 'What do you mean?'

'Well, it occurred to me that as I'm not going to be back at work for a few days yet, I could perhaps take him out and about a bit—with your permission, of course. You could come along, too, if the doctors think you're fit enough. I could take him to the park perhaps in the first instance. And then maybe if he's all right with that we could go further afield on another day…perhaps next Saturday? I was thinking of a trip to Loch Lomond…nothing strenuous, just a chance to show him the sights. It's not too far away from here. I could get hold of a wheelchair and take him around a bit, if you like.'

Connor's mother was obviously delighted by the suggestion. 'I'm pretty sure that the doctors won't release me just yet—I've already asked. There's no reason why Connor shouldn't go, though.' She looked at her son and asked, 'What do you think? Would you like to do that?'

'Wow, yes, you bet,' the boy said with enthusiasm. He glanced across the room at Rebecca. 'Will you come with us, Becca?' he asked. 'Please, say that you will.'

Rebecca gave a cautious nod. 'If that's what you would like,' she said, 'then yes, I will, to the loch at least.' She didn't want to let Connor down, but even as she said it she realised that it meant she and Craig would be going on this outing together. How would Craig feel about that?

'That is,' she added, 'if it's all right with Craig and your mother.'

'I'd be really pleased if you would go along with him,' Connor's mother put in. 'You've been so good with him up to now, and I'd feel that he was in capable hands.'

'OK, then.' Rebecca turned to look questioningly at Craig.

'That's fine by me,' he murmured.

He smiled, but she had no idea what he was thinking. It occurred to her that she had landed herself with two outings in quick succession, and somehow, from the glimmer that arose in his eyes as he glanced towards her, it felt very much as though she was playing with fire.

'Anyway,' Craig said, turning back to Connor, 'it's good to see you looking so well. You've made my day.' He paused. 'Unfortunately, though, we have to leave you now, because we need to be somewhere else in a very short time. I'll come and pick you up tomorrow afternoon to take you to the park.'

They finished saying their goodbyes, and once they were in the corridor outside the ward, Craig turned towards the lifts and Rebecca hurried alongside him. She wasn't sure how she felt about these hours that she would be spending with him, and part of her wondered whether she ought to be finding herself somewhere to live, instead of planning leisure activities with someone who might turn out to be a wolf in sheep's clothing. Why was he doing so much to help her?

He wasn't giving her time to think about any of that,

though. 'I thought we might collect your cases and then go
and take a look at the village around Port Charlotte,' he
murmured. 'I'm sure you know it well but I haven't been
in a while and it's a pretty little place with all those white-
washed houses and the rocky coves. I used to go there as
a child with my family. My brother liked to watch the birds
in flight around Islay, and I loved finding rock pools and
searching for crabs.'

She smiled. 'Just hearing you talk about it makes me
feel as though I'm there already. I've dreamed of it. I can't
wait.'

It wasn't too long before the dream became fact, and
they were walking along that picturesque part of the island.
The ferry trip had been a restful, happy experience. They
had stood together by the rail of the ship ferry and looked
out over the water, delighting in the beautiful sight of the
islands as they'd passed by. Craig had slipped his arm
around her waist, drawing her against him, and even with
that simple gesture he had managed to turn her body to
flame. She had been far too strongly aware of him.

Even so, she had tried hard to ignore the wayward response of her nervous system as he'd pointed out the
various landmarks.

'It's all coming back to me just how much I miss this
place,' she murmured when they were back on dry land,
and she was able to drink in the breathtaking sights and
sounds all around her.

'It was a good thing that you sent your cases over here,
then,' Craig said with a smile. 'It gave you just the excuse
that you needed to come and visit the place.'

She nodded agreement. 'Now that I'm here, I really don't want to leave.'

'I know...I can see that. It's clear as crystal in your expression and in the way your mouth softens when you gaze around you.' He looked at her, his expression a mixture of understanding and mild amusement. 'There's something captivating about that look in your eyes. I imagine many a man would want to have you look at him like that, in the hungry way you devour this place with your glance, as though it's everything in the world that you could ever want.'

She laughed, even as her cheeks filled with gentle heat. 'Like I said, I've always felt as though coming here was like coming home.'

'Perhaps you'll do that before too long?' His glance was quizzical, and she responded with a light shrug.

'Maybe, when Heather is strong enough...and provided that I have a job to come home to.'

They spent an hour or so walking along the beach, stopping every now and again to watch the waves lap the shoreline, and Craig took time out to skim pebbles out over the water.

They stopped for a while at a little café, taking the air out on the decking and looking out to sea as they sipped ice-cold drinks.

Rebecca bought herself a slender watch from a gift shop in the coastal village, and realised that time was slipping by. 'I suppose we ought to be starting back,' she murmured wistfully.

'You're right,' Craig agreed. 'If we leave now, we should be able to make it back to the ferry in good time.'

They walked back to the car, ready to drive towards the port once more. 'About the job,' he said, as he slid behind the wheel and set the car in motion. 'I've arranged for you to come in to A and E and talk things through with the consultant in charge. There's a position waiting for you if you want it…only it's with the children's area of A and E. I don't know how you feel about that. I know you were beginning to feel that working with very sick children can be too upsetting at times.'

'Is that the only job on offer?'

He nodded. 'It's the post that needs to be filled immediately. There should be another one coming up in a week or so, but that one would be a permanent position, and I'm not sure how you would feel about taking that on.'

Rebecca made a face. 'I don't really have a choice, do I? I need to stay near my aunt, and I've worked with children for a long time, so I dare say I'm best suited to that, skill-wise. I'll go along and talk with the consultant.'

'Good. I'm glad about that. I think you've made a wise decision.'

A few minutes later they arrived at the ferry terminal, and he drove the car into the holding bay.

Craig's mobile phone began to ring as they climbed out of the car. He checked the name of the caller. 'You go on ahead,' he said. 'I'll just answer this and then we'll sit out on the upper deck, if you like.'

She nodded, and slowly started for the stairs. 'Cheryl,' she heard him say, 'I didn't know that you were back in Scotland. I thought you were supposed to be in Yorkshire until Saturday week?'

Rebecca didn't hear the reply, but she recognised the

instant when his voice lowered in tone and became husky and affectionate. 'It's all right,' he said. 'There's no need for you to worry. Everything's fine. How did the meeting go? Will you be going back there again?'

There was a momentary silence while he listened, and then his voice dropped once again. 'You don't have to do that. It's going to be fine, sweetheart, believe me.'

Rebecca realised that he had dropped behind and that he was no longer following her up the stairs. His tone was gentle and coaxing, and it was gradually fading as she made her way to the upper deck.

Who was on the other end of the line? Clearly, it was a woman, and someone he seemed to care for very much. He had called her sweetheart.

Rebecca's heart began to set up a heavy thud, thud, beating like a sorrowful drum. Why did it bother her so much that he was stopping to have a private chat with a woman who obviously meant a great deal to him?

But she knew the answer to that already, didn't she? She had only known him for a short time, but it had been time enough for her to lose her heart to him. She was a fool, an idiot. Would she never learn?

CHAPTER NINE

'I'M WORRIED about this baby,' Rebecca said with a frown, glancing at the nurse who was assisting her. 'She was born prematurely, and that has caused quite a few problems already. Now it looks as though the pressure's rising within the blood vessels of her heart. She's very weak.'

She ran the cup of her stethoscope over the infant's chest, listening intently for a while. 'I can hear a heart murmur, and together with the bluish tinge around her mouth and the fast rate of her breathing, things aren't looking too good.' Her voice took on a thread of urgency. 'We need to get the paediatric cardiologist down here so that he can take a look at her.'

Helen nodded. 'I'll give him a call right away, but I know he's with another patient just now, so it may be a while before he's able to come down here. I'll keep our Dr Bradshaw informed in the meantime. He's in charge of the day-to-day running of the A and E department at the moment.'

'OK…just so long as we've set things in motion. I'm going to order an echocardiograph so that we can see the heart in action, and we'll get an X-ray, too.' She frowned.

'I've a feeling that this infant is going to need surgery fairly soon. We can use medication to help her along in the meantime, but I don't think that it's going to be enough.'

'If it's a question of surgery,' Helen said, 'she may have to be transferred to the Royal. They have all the facilities for specialist treatment over there.' She paused, thinking things through. 'I'll break it to the mother as gently as I can. She must know that her child has a heart condition, but perhaps she wasn't aware of quite how serious it is. This is going to come as a shock.'

Rebecca nodded. 'I'll come along with you to speak to her, if you like. I might be able to answer some of the questions she's bound to ask.'

'Thanks. That would be good.' Helen made a small adjustment to the oxygen delivery equipment and then straightened up. 'It's great to have you working here with us, Rebecca. I'm really glad that Craig persuaded you to join us. We've been struggling along here short-handed for quite a while, and you're perfect for the unit. I'm just sorry that your post is only temporary. You're really good with the children.' Helen frowned. 'Craig said he wasn't sure that you would go for it.'

Rebecca gave her a brief smile. 'I was working in paediatrics in my last position, and that's probably why Craig thought of me in the first place. It's just that I was looking for something different… In my last job I found the work could be more upsetting at times than I expected.'

'That's true enough.' Helen was serious for a moment. 'Any work with sick children can be heartbreaking at times, but I suppose I comfort myself by thinking about the little ones we manage to save…and there are lots and lots of those. It's always good to see them recover and flourish.'

Rebecca nodded. 'And we'll do all that we can for this little one.' She looked down at the tiny infant and reached out with a finger to stroke her small hand. The baby's fingers curled around hers as though she recognised a friend and protector, and Rebecca smiled softly. 'I'm here, baby. We'll do our very best to see you through this, I promise.'

Helen went to make the phone call and came back a moment or two later, saying, 'Dr Bradshaw will be down as soon as he can make it. He said to monitor Chloe on a regular basis and consult with Craig if there are any problems in the meantime.'

'I'll do that.' Rebecca frowned. 'Do we know where Craig is right now? Is he actually on the premises?'

Helen nodded. 'I saw him in the office earlier. He said he had to call Cheryl to make sure she was coping all right with the move to her new place, and then he was going to be spending some time in the trauma unit.'

'Oh, I see.' Rebecca's stomach made an uncomfortable twist. Cheryl. After the boat trip from Islay, it had taken her some time to get over the shock of hearing Craig speaking to the unknown woman with such affection. How deeply was he involved with her?

'I've heard him talking on the phone to someone called Cheryl,' Rebecca murmured. 'Is she a girlfriend, perhaps, or a relative?' She chided herself inwardly for asking, but the question had been tormenting her for several days now. Craig hadn't volunteered any information.

'A girlfriend, I think. At any rate, they've known each

other for a long time and they seem to be very close. When she found out that he'd been involved in a helicopter crash she called here to try to find out what had happened to him. She was distraught and we did our best to comfort her, but it was difficult because we weren't sure what was happening ourselves.'

'That must have been terrible for all of you.'

Helen nodded. 'It was. We all think the world of him. I don't know how we would have gone on if he had been hurt, or worse.'

'He's resourceful, to say the least,' Rebecca told her. 'If anyone was going to come through it, he was.'

She was still trying to take in the fact that the woman Cheryl was dear to Craig. Just how close were they? Craig hadn't said a word on the subject, and why should he, after all? What business was it of hers, anyway? Cheryl had been an established part of his life way before *she* had come along, hadn't she?

Rebecca had no claim on him. And there was no point in arguing that Craig had kissed her, and made her feel as though she was special, because she had partly been to blame for what had gone on between them. She was the one who had turned to him. He was a man, with primal instincts, and who would have blamed him for acting on them?

Tormenting herself this way was doing her no good at all. She tried to push those thoughts out of her head and said quietly, 'So he isn't out with the emergency service?'

Helen shook her head. 'He alternates with the helicopter service and A and E. Usually he spends three or four weeks with us and then a week out on call. I think he prefers it that way because it means he gets variety in the job.'

'I can see how he would choose that.' Rebecca stiffened her shoulders. 'I'll go and find him and let him know what's happening. If the infant has to go to another hospital, he'll need to know the arrangements.'

As things turned out, though, it was Dr Bradshaw who set up the transfer. 'I've spoken with the team at the Royal,' he said, looking from Craig to Rebecca, 'and they'll be standing by to receive the infant into their neonatal unit.' His mouth twisted a fraction. 'Of course, it would have been better all round if we could have waited until the baby was stronger before she underwent surgery, but her condition will only deteriorate if it's left. It's just a question now of arranging transport.'

He sent Rebecca an enquiring glance. 'She'll need to be accompanied on the journey, and since you've been taking care of her, you would be the logical choice to stay with her. Would you be prepared to do that?'

'Of course.' Rebecca nodded, and then pulled herself up. 'We are talking ambulance transport, aren't we? She won't be going by helicopter, will she?'

Dr Bradshaw frowned. 'I suppose the helicopter would be quicker.' He glanced at Craig. 'I don't know how you feel about that, given what happened. But you're not on call this week, are you?'

Craig shook his head. 'I'm not, but I had a word with the pilot earlier on and it looks as though his schedule is pretty full right now.' He sent Rebecca a thoughtful glance. 'Going by road will probably be the smoothest course of action. We can use one of the dedicated neonatal ambulances.'

'That's what we'll do, then,' Dr Bradshaw said, and Rebecca gave a silent sigh of relief. It wouldn't have been a good start if she'd refused an assignment at the very beginning of her time here, would it? Dr Bradshaw appeared to be an understanding kind of man, but all the same she didn't want to seem as though she was lacking in confidence.

She glanced at Craig. Had he deliberately stepped in to rescue her? She sent him a look of gratitude, and he must have read her thoughts because he smiled in return.

'I'll help get things organised,' he said. 'We'll check up on the breathing and monitoring equipment and set up a communications link with both hospitals. Since this is Rebecca's first transport with our hospital, it would probably be as well if I go along with her and go over all the details of the special equipment carried on board.' He checked his watch. 'I'm off duty as of five minutes ago, so it won't cause a problem back here.'

Dr Bradshaw nodded. 'That sounds like a good idea. I'll let the ambulance staff know what's happening.' He smiled briefly. 'I'll leave you both to get on with it, then. Perhaps you should stay long enough over there to advise the team on any issues that might crop up. It could be practical to follow the course of the operation and report back to us here, as we'll be following up on her after-care.'

'OK.' Rebecca made a quick check of the infant's chart. 'I've explained to the mother that Chloe is going to have surgery to close the ductus arteriosus, and that will hopefully improve the circulation of her blood and make sure that her lungs receive adequate oxygen.'

'She's very young, and still a touch underweight, so she'll more than likely need intensive care for a while afterwards,' Craig remarked. 'The Royal is probably the best place for that initially, but it's a shame that the mother and child have to be separated this way.'

Rebecca nodded agreement as she began to gather together all the paperwork that she would need for the journey. 'This was never going to be a good situation.' She felt better, knowing that Craig would be going along with her, but it wasn't because she didn't feel able to cope with the demands of the job. It was simply that having him around gave a lift to her spirits.

'How is your aunt getting on?' Craig asked when Dr Bradshaw had moved away. 'The last time we had a chance to talk, you said she had recovered some of the feeling in her leg.'

'That's right, she has.' She started to prepare Chloe for the transfer, collecting together all the equipment they would need and making sure that everything was in place. 'It was a wonderful moment, and it gave us hope that things will turn out all right. Heather was a bit tearful, but clearly happy and relieved.'

'I'll call in and see her when I'm on a lunch-break,' Craig said. 'She seems a plucky character. It's always a good sign when you get some recovery in the first few weeks after a stroke. The first six months especially are crucial, and this initial development has to be good news.'

'Yes, it is. I think she'll still need to be in hospital for some time to come, though, and that means I'll have to stay close by her for several weeks yet.'

She frowned. Living in Craig's home had been a lifeline for her up to now, but it wasn't going to be an option for much longer, was it? He was a thoughtful and considerate man, a wonderful person to be with, but with every moment that she spent with him she found herself becoming more deeply drawn to him.

It wouldn't do. She was far too conscious of him already and each day that passed found her wanting something more from her tenuous relationship with him, a deeper, stronger bond that would perhaps bind them together.

It was a reckless longing, and her survival instincts weren't kicking in. They had let her down before, and she ought to know that no good could come of her involvement with him. Why should this be an exception to the rule?

'I'll start looking for a place of my own just as soon as I get some time off,' she said. 'With starting this new job and spending time with Connor and Heather, I haven't had a chance to get myself together yet.'

He walked with her to the ambulance bay. 'You don't have to move out of my home,' he said. 'Things have been working out all right so far, haven't they?'

'Yes, they have.' All too well, she reflected. 'But I need my independence. I need to feel that I'm in charge of my own destiny.'

He frowned. 'I'm not altogether sure that I understand what you're getting at, but you have to know I don't see a problem with you staying. My home is yours for as long as you need it.'

She made a soft smile. 'Thanks. You're too generous by

half, and if you're not careful, women will be queuing up to take advantage of your good nature.'

His eyes widened, his brows making an exaggerated upward lift. 'Really? Do you think so? That sounds altogether promising. I must look into that.'

She gave him a playful punch. 'Let's get on with it.'

'Yes, ma'am. Lead the way.'

He stayed close by her in the ambulance, watching over the infant and generally checking that there were no adverse signs.

'She's tiny, isn't she, such a fragile little human being?'

Rebecca nodded. 'She hasn't been feeding well. I've tried a few times to bottle-feed her, but it's a long job.' She smiled. 'Not that I mind at all. It's lovely to be able to hold her and give her a cuddle while she drinks her milk.'

Craig's gaze moved over her. 'Would you like a family of your own someday?'

'Yes, I think I would.' Her mouth straightened. 'I don't see it happening any time soon, though.'

'Why is that?'

Rebecca gave an awkward shrug. 'Perhaps because I haven't met anyone who I could rely on to be there for me through thick and thin, and somehow I don't think it's ever going to happen. I'd have to be sure that I had met the right man, and I'm not convinced that he exists.'

That wasn't strictly true, of course. The one man she would consider a perfect choice to be the father of her children was sitting right beside her, but he was accounted for, wasn't he?

Craig was silent for a moment or two. Then he said

soberly, 'You've been hurt in the past. It will take time for you to get over that.'

'Maybe.' She frowned as one of the monitors started bleeping, and she saw that the baby was becoming restless. 'Her heart rate is up,' she said quickly, 'and her breathing is laboured. It looks as though her lungs are congested.'

'Another dose of diuretic would help to clear some of the fluid.'

'And a bronchodilator would be useful, too.' Rebecca started to administer the medication, adding softly, 'We can at least keep her condition stable until she has the surgery.'

'If that isn't enough, you could always try giving her an inhaled steroid. A small dose wouldn't do any harm and could make a lot of difference.'

'I'll keep it in mind.' Rebecca sighed, watching the child closely. 'You hang on in there, little one,' she murmured. 'There's not long for you to wait now. We'll be there soon.'

She was right, and just a short time later the ambulance pulled up in the bay outside the Royal. A team was waiting to receive the infant, and within minutes she was being whisked into the treatment room in preparation for her trip to the operating theatre.

'It's going to be a while before we have any news of how she's doing,' Craig said some time later when the baby was ready for surgery. 'Shall we go and have some lunch and then maybe take a slow walk by the river? It would be better than hanging around, waiting. I've left my mobile phone number with the sister in charge, so that she can stay in touch with us.'

'OK. That sounds like a good idea.'

They ate a light lunch in the hospital restaurant and

then set off for the river that flowed through a nearby park. It was a beautiful summer's day, with not a cloud in the sky, and Rebecca appreciated the chance to breathe in the fresh air and gaze at the colourful rhododendrons that flowered in profusion. They wandered along the riverbank, watching the water drift gently by, and she even managed to glimpse an occasional fish darting about in the shallows.

'You must have been here before,' she murmured, watching Craig as he headed towards the bridge. 'You seem to know your way around pretty well.'

He nodded. 'Yes, I used to come down here when I worked at the Royal. I did some of my training around here, so I'm used to visiting all the local places of interest.'

Had he come here with Cheryl? It was on the tip of her tongue to ask, but she resisted the urge, and then he took her hand in his and led her over the bridge, pointing out the swans in the reeds on the far side of the water.

'They don't have a care in the world, do they?' he murmured. 'I used to come here and gaze out over the water from time to time. It made me feel peaceful inside whenever I'd had a bad day.'

She glanced at him, her gaze drinking in his strong features, the confident way he stood, tall and strong, looking out over the landscape. 'You never give the impression that anything bothers you,' she said. 'You always seem to brush off any difficulties that crop up, but I expect you keep it bottled up inside and hide your feelings from everyone around.'

'We all have bad times,' he said. 'The key is to find ways to get over them.'

'Is that why you brought me here?' she asked softly. 'So that I could forget my troubles?'

'I guess it is.' He gave a half-smile. 'You've had a hard time lately, with one thing and another, and I thought you could do with a break. Islay isn't the only place where you might find peace and calm, you know. You just have to know where to look.'

'You're right. This is lovely, and I'm glad you brought me here.' She liked the way he held her hand in his, his fingers wrapped firmly around hers, his arm keeping her close by his side. His actions made it seem as though he cared for her, and that made her feel warm inside. But by allowing herself to fall for him, wasn't she setting herself up to be hurt? What was she to make of him? Was he everything she thought he was, or was there a side to him that he kept hidden from her? It grieved her that she didn't know, and it hurt that she wasn't able to put her trust in him.

'Perhaps we should start back,' he said on a reluctant note after a while. They had been strolling along the pathways of the park for around half an hour, and Rebecca was beginning to relax in his company. She didn't want to go back to normality, to the rush of everyday life, but of course there was no avoiding reality. Chloe would be coming out of surgery by now, and she wanted to know how things had gone.

She had been able to snatch a few moments alone with Craig, and they had been blissful while they lasted, but she was all too conscious that they might not be hers to treasure.

They might have been stolen from someone else.

CHAPTER TEN

'So YOU had to leave the wee bairn at the hospital?' Heather asked in the halting tone that Rebecca was becoming used to by now. She was sitting in a chair by the side of her bed, trying to exercise her leg, but it was a slow and difficult process, and Rebecca was standing by, ready to lend a hand by directing her movements.

'Yes, we did, poor little thing. She went straight into Intensive Care, and we were hoping that she would be fit enough to travel within a day or two, but it doesn't look as though that's going to happen. The doctors are worried about complications with her lungs and blood pressure.' Rebecca's mouth turned down sadly. 'She's so tiny. Her mother must be beside herself with worry.'

'Aye, it can't be easy.' Heather struggled from her sitting position to move her foot forward and back, but her face suddenly drained of colour, and Rebecca could see that she was exhausted by her efforts. She carefully helped her to settle back against her cushions.

'I think that's probably enough exercise for today,' she told her aunt. 'You've done really well.'

Her aunt sighed, looking thoroughly disgruntled. 'I don't feel as though I'm getting anywhere.'

Rebecca smiled. 'I know it might seem like nothing very much to you, but you've come on tremendously in these last few days. Your speech has improved by leaps and bounds, and you're gaining strength in your limbs every time you exercise. Don't be discouraged. You're doing fine.'

'You're a good girl. I know you're trying to cheer me up.' Heather sent her a brief, assessing look. 'How are things with you? Are you still living with that good-looking doctor who comes around every day?'

She was using hand gestures to help make her speech understood, and Rebecca laughed. 'You make it sound positively sinful. I'm not living with him, not really. It was just that I had nowhere else to go at the time. As it turned out, we work different shift patterns and I haven't really seen an awful lot of him back at the house. I see more of him here, at work. And, anyway, I'm looking around for a place of my own, somewhere near the hospital.'

Heather was thoughtful for a second or two. 'There's my parent's old cottage out of town, here on the mainland. It's not up to much and it's a bit run down, but you could see what you think.' She indicated her bag on the bedside table. 'Help me find the key.'

Rebecca did as she asked, and Heather used her good arm to rummage for the key. 'I knew I still had it somewhere,' she said at last, handing it over to Rebecca with a lopsided grin of triumph. 'You take it.'

'Thanks.' Rebecca remembered the old cottage from years ago when she had visited occasionally with her mother when her grandparents had still been alive. It was small and very basic, but at least it would be a roof over her head. She pushed the key into her pocket and concentrated on making her aunt comfortable.

Heather looked as though she was washed out from her efforts, and Rebecca tucked a blanket around her legs and gently patted her shoulder. 'You should try to get some rest. I have to go back to work now—I'm on callout with the ambulance—but I'll drop by to see you later, when I get back.'

Heather nodded, her eyelids already closing, and Rebecca quietly left the room.

Going out with the ambulance had been Dr Bradshaw's idea. He thought it would be a good way for her to reacquaint herself with the whole area of emergency work, and at the same time allow her to get to know everyone who was involved in their patients' care.

Since Craig had helped her out with the baby's transfer, he'd decided it would be a good idea for him to go on keeping an eye on her for a while. She didn't have any objection to being watched over—after all, she was new to the job—but she was finding it hard being thrust into Craig's company all the time. The way she felt about him, it would have been easier for her if there had been some distance between them.

'We've had a call about a road accident,' Craig said, coming over to her as she was flicking through files at the nurses' station some time later. 'It's a major accident on the main highway, several cars have collided, and they're calling for as many doctors to attend as possible.'

'I'll get my bag.' She sent him a hurried glance. 'Do we know how the accident happened?'

'From what I've managed to piece together, it looks as though someone was trying to overtake a slow-moving vehicle, and another driver had to take evasive action to avoid hitting him. That caused a third driver to swerve, and his car overturned. Then someone went into the back of him. I don't think that was the end of it.'

Rebecca winced, gathering together all her belongings and hurrying along beside him. 'That sounds really bad. Do the police have the road closed off by now?'

'Yes. We're clear to go in.' By that time they had arrived at the ambulance bay, and the driver already had the engine of the vehicle revved up and ready to go.

The paramedic slid in beside them and then they were off, heading towards the scene of the accident.

Rebecca glanced at Craig as they sped away. He wasn't saying anything and he looked as though he was preoccupied, his jaw taut, his gaze fixed on the passing landscape, but she doubted he was seeing any of it.

'Are you OK?' she asked.

It was a second or two before he realised that she had spoken to him. 'Yes, I'm fine,' he said, and when he looked away again his face held a shuttered expression and she thought better of asking him any more questions.

'Everyone has their own way of psyching themselves up to attend emergencies,' the paramedic confided. 'You don't know what you're going to come up against, and it's not like receiving patients in a hospital. It can be disorientating if you're not ready for it.'

Rebecca nodded. He was trying to be helpful, and she

knew that what he was saying was right in some instances, but she didn't think that was the case with Craig. He was always prepared, always ready for any eventuality. This occasion was somehow different.

'Is this an accident black spot?' she asked as they drew close to their destination. The road curved at this point, and there were areas where the highway up ahead might not be clearly visible to a driver. Perhaps Craig had been here before.

The paramedic was nodding. 'Yes, there are often problems along this stretch, particularly in winter,' he said quietly. 'There was an especially nasty accident up here a couple of years ago. I didn't attend back then, but I heard about it. A young man was caught up in the carnage and died from his injuries. It turned out he was only there by chance, on his way back from a job interview and he'd taken a detour to miss the snowdrifts that were pilng up on the other road. It was very sad.'

The ambulance came to a stop, and they all left the vehicle, taking time to look around and assess the surrounding area before moving to where they might be needed. There was wreckage of crumpled cars all around, and there were police vehicles parked at intervals, with lights flashing and sirens blaring. The smell of petrol pervaded the air, and there was smoke coming from one of the car engines. Firemen were already on hand, and an ambulance crew was attending to some of the injured people.

At least it was only late afternoon, and the sky was clear, giving them enough light so that they would be able to see clearly for the next hour or so. Craig was already striding forward and Rebecca followed him, going over to talk to the doctor who was leading the team. 'Where do you want me to go?' she asked, when Craig had moved away in the direction of the overturned vehicle.

'We have a woman with head and chest injuries in the middle vehicle,' the doctor told her. 'She's been stabilised, but we've had to wait while the fire service try to release her. Once they give you the go-ahead, you need to assess her condition once again and prepare her for transport. Then there's a man with a broken arm over there by the side of the road. He's been assessed briefly, and given pain medication, but he'll need a splint to protect the fracture before he's ready to travel.'

'All right. I'll see to it.'

Rebecca made a hurried examination of the young woman, and established that she was receiving adequate ventilation through intubation. She was unconscious and bleeding from a chest wound, and once she had been freed from the wreckage Rebecca was able to apply a pressure pad to the injured area to reduce the bleeding.

She quickly gave the woman intravenous fluids to make up for blood loss, and then briefly checked her responses. The head injury was a worry, but all she could do for now was to ensure that she was sent on her way to hospital in the shortest possible time.

The paramedic was working alongside her, and now he said, 'I'll immobilise the cervical spine, and then we can ease her into the scoop stretcher.'

Rebecca nodded. 'Yes, we've done all we can here.'

When the patient had been transferred to the ambulance, she went to attend to the man with the broken arm.

Once he had been made comfortable and was passed into the care of the ambulance crew, she went to look for Craig.

She found him taking care of a man who was trapped in the overturned vehicle. The fire crew had cut part of it away so that he could reach the patient more easily. 'Is there anything I can do to help?' she asked.

Craig sent her a fleeting glance. His face was ashen and his answer came through tight lips. 'See if you can do something to restore the circulation to his foot. His ankle was wedged under the metalwork, and the firemen have only just managed to free it.'

Rebecca knelt down to find a comfortable position where she could treat the man. He was in his early thirties, and he looked as though the life was draining from him. She turned her attention to his ankle, noting the abnormal dislocation that had turned his foot through a ninety-degree angle, and said anxiously, 'How's he doing apart from that?'

'He's not good. I think the injury to his chest penetrated the heart wall and it's causing a pericardial tamponade. The fluid is building up and compressing the heart so that his circulation is failing.'

That was bad news, and possibly the worst, because few people survived that kind of injury out on the road. She concentrated on her own task, placing her hands over the man's foot and trying to pull it back into a more normal state. It shifted into place with a loud click. Then she pressed her lips together and asked cautiously, 'How long has he been like that?'

'Since I arrived here. I've been trying to stem the bleeding.'

Rebecca searched her bag for a splint that she could use on the ankle. 'I've done what I can to straighten the foot, but the circulation isn't improving a great deal.' It probably wouldn't until his heart was working properly once more, and that eventuality looked to be some way off.

She taped the splint in place and then stared anxiously at Craig. He was determined to help this man to survive, but the odds were surely stacked against him. The man's neck veins were distended, but his blood pressure was dangerously low and his heart sounds had decreased. He was hovering between life and death, and Craig was doing everything that he could to save him.

What was it that drove him on where others would have conceded defeat?

He was drawing up a needle, and she guessed that he was getting ready to insert it into the pericardial sac around the man's heart, so that he could withdraw the fluid that was causing the build-up of pressure.

'How can you do that without proper guidance... without equipment?' She was faintly shocked by his daring, and her voice wavered. 'We're out in the open here. How do you know that you can position the needle correctly?'

'I'll use the portable ECG machine. I can attach the leads to the needle with a clip and use the information from the monitor to help guide me. Anyway, the way I see it, we don't have any choice. If I do nothing, he'll die for sure.'

He was already infiltrating the area with anaesthetic. His mouth set in a grim line and he continued with the rest of the procedure without further ado. Rebecca watched with bated breath as he pushed in the needle and inserted a guide wire. Then he removed the needle and replaced it with a catheter.

She quickly searched in the medical bag for a container, and handed it to him so that he could fix the other end of the tube in place and allow the fluid to be collected.

'What about his other injuries?' she asked. 'He's obviously had a sharp knock to the head.'

'I'm doing what I can to keep the intracranial pressure from rising. We just have to take one thing at a time and hope for the best.'

'Is there anything I can do?'

'Help me get him onto the stretcher. We need to keep him as still as possible on the way to the hospital.'

They worked together with the paramedic to slide the man into the scoop, and then Craig made sure that all the various tubes and drains were in place before he allowed the paramedics to take him away.

'OK, let's get him to hospital as quickly as possible,' he said. He climbed up into the ambulance and seated himself alongside the patient. Rebecca went with him. There were no more patients left who needed attention, and she readied herself to watch over this man and do what she could to see him through.

'Where's the paramedic who came with us?' she asked, looking around.

'He's been seconded to another vehicle,' Craig said. 'The other team was struggling with a badly injured man and they needed an extra pair of hands.'

'That's unusual, isn't it?'

He shrugged. 'We're all going in the same direction. Besides, there are two of us.'

They set off along the road towards the hospital, but they hadn't gone more than five minutes into the journey when the monitor started to bleep. 'His heart's slipped into an irregular, chaotic rhythm,' she said, and immediately Craig was on his feet.

He started to charge the defibrillator. 'Clear,' he said. Rebecca stood back. He applied the paddles to the man's chest and then waited a moment. 'Charging.' He waited until the machine was ready, and then he applied the paddles again.

It wasn't working, and Rebecca bit her lip. 'Craig,' she said after a while, 'you've done everything you can. He's gone into cardiac arrest and I'm not sure that anything is going to work. He's too weak and he's lost a lot of blood.'

Craig's face set in a mask of determination. 'I'm not giving up.' He drew up a syringe of epinephrine and plunged it directly into the man's heart. Then he charged up the defibrillator once more. 'Ready,' he said. 'Clear.'

There was a momentary lull. 'We have a sinus rhythm,' Rebecca said in wonder. Her eyes widened as she gazed at Craig. 'You've brought him back. You've done it.'

He checked the monitors, then replaced the paddles and sat down as though there was nothing left inside him, as though all the energy had fizzled out of him. Rebecca went to sit beside him and then she wrapped her arms around him and gave him a hug. She rested her cheek against his, and after a moment or two she felt his trembling response. His head moved and his mouth searched for hers, and then he was kissing her, a long, hard kiss, as though her touch had been the catalyst to set free all the pent-up emotion that had been dammed up inside him.

Rebecca kissed him in return, her lips tingling, her head reeling with sensation, but after a moment or two sanity returned and she broke away from him. She was breathing raggedly, stunned by the vibrancy of that kiss, but even though it had shaken her to the core, she felt that she couldn't let it go on. She didn't understand what was driving him, and he clearly didn't know what he was doing. Besides, they had an injured man to watch over.

She swiftly checked the patient and made certain that all was as well as could be. 'You saved him,' she said huskily. 'He went right to the brink and you made sure that he stayed with us.'

He made no reply and she stared at him for a second or two. 'You haven't been yourself since we set out this afternoon,' she said. 'Is there something wrong—something special about this trip?'

Craig replied. 'I have been here before.' He gave a deep sigh, a kind of hoarse rumble that started in the back of his throat. 'There was another accident a couple of years ago at that same bend in the road. It was a horrible winter's evening, and the road conditions were icy. Cars had piled up. I was called out to attend to the accident, and I went along, thinking that it would be business as usual.'

He gave a shudder. 'These things are never easy, but this was the worst. I found that my best friend was in one of the vehicles. His car had overturned, just like the one back there.'

He pulled in a deep breath to steady himself. 'I worked with him for more than an hour while we waited for the fire crew to free him. I did everything I could to try to save him, but it simply wasn't enough. He died, and somehow I've had to try to live with that ever since. They told me that no one could have brought him back, that his injuries were too severe, but I had to try.'

She placed her hand over his. 'I'm so sorry,' she said huskily. 'That must have been terrible for you. Going back there today must have brought it all back.' She looked at him. He appeared haggard, as though he was devastated by events. 'You look shattered. Will you be all right? I can take over here for you. It's getting very late. Perhaps you would be better off at home.'

His mouth made an odd shape. 'You should know me better than that by now. I'm not going home. I'm going to see this through. This man is going to survive, and I'm going to be there to see to it.'

Rebecca let go of his hand as the ambulance drew up into the bay by the hospital. The trauma team came out to receive the patient, and she went along with them, filling them in on the details of his condition.

Craig was walking by the side of the trolley, his attention fixed on the monitors, and she knew that he would not leave the man's side. They would have to prise him away, and she knew enough of the way this unit worked to know that no one would attempt any such thing.

She waited at the hospital until the patient came down from Theatre some hours later. She watched as he was wheeled away into a recovery ward, and she stepped out from an isolated side ward to follow Craig's progress as he walked towards her. He was wearing full theatre garb, and she guessed that they had let him scrub in to watch proceedings.

She let her gaze trail over him. 'How is he doing?' she asked.

His face broke into a tired smile. 'He's OK. I think he's going to pull through.'

'I'm so glad.' She looked up at him. 'I checked up on the woman I helped as well and she's also come through surgery OK.'

He nodded and wrapped his arms around her, holding her tight. 'It's been a long day,' he said. 'Let's go home.'

'Home.' She echoed the word softly. 'That sounds wonderful, but I have to say you look as though you could tumble into bed and fall straight to sleep.'

'You're right, I could.' He looked down at her and smiled. 'Maybe you should get a good night's rest, too. We have a date tomorrow, remember?'

A date? A line indented her brow. For a moment she had to think what he meant, and then she realised that tomorrow was Saturday. 'Connor…and Loch Lomond. I hadn't given it a thought since this morning. Do you think he'll still want to go?'

'I am absolutely sure of it. He enjoyed his trip to the park when we went, and he's talked of nothing else since. We had better be on our toes tomorrow, because he'll be fidgeting to get out and about again. Sick as he is, that boy has a lot of drive.'

'Then I guess it's a case of Loch Lomond, here we come,' she said with a grin.

Saturday dawned, a bright and beautiful day, and Rebecca was glad of that. It had been a long time since she'd been to the shores of Loch Lomond, and she was looking forward to it, all the more so because Craig would be there with her. Would it be such a dreadful thing if she were to throw caution to the wind for a short time?

Craig was up with the lark, fit and energised and ready to go. Rebecca walked into the kitchen, yawning as she tried to shake off the aftermath of sleep, but she stopped suddenly in the doorway, looking him over.

He was dressed in black denims that fitted him to perfection and a sports shirt that was open at the neck to reveal a glimpse of his lightly bronzed skin. His hair gleamed, jet black with iridescent highlights, still damp from the shower.

'I can see that you're ready to go,' she said. 'You'll have to give me a minute to grab some toast. I'm running a bit late.'

He ran his gaze over her from head to toe. 'I'd say it was worth it,' he said, a smile playing around his lips. 'You fit those jeans as though you've been poured into them, and as for the top you're wearing…'

'Perhaps we shouldn't go there,' she murmured, stopping him in his tracks. 'This is a kind of family outing we're preparing for.' Even so, she was pleased that he liked the way she looked. She flicked back the burnished mass of her hair and helped herself to toast and apricot preserve.

'Is that all you're having?' he asked, raising a dark brow.

She nodded. 'It'll do me for now. I don't want to keep Connor waiting.'

She was still buoyed up by the fact that they were going to spend a good few hours together. It wasn't really a date, of course, but she could pretend, couldn't she? And even though they weren't going to be alone, she was fizzing happily with the thought of walking along the shores of the loch with him.

CHAPTER ELEVEN

'THIS is so cool!' Connor exclaimed. He was peering through the deck rail out over Loch Lomond, while Rebecca pointed out the mountains in the distance. He smiled happily. 'I love being out here.'

'That's the general idea,' Craig told him, his tone cheerful. 'We thought you might appreciate a boat trip across the loch. It's calm and clear today, so you can look out at all the scenery.'

'I like the islands,' Connor remarked, his eyes shining. 'They're beautiful, and you can see for miles around.' He shifted in his wheelchair, tilting his head to look up at Craig. 'Do we have to go straight back to the hospital when we come off the boat? I don't want to go back yet.'

Craig shook his head. 'We can look around the village for a while, if you like. I don't want to keep you out too long in case it's tiring for you, but there are some quaint little gift shops and pretty stone-built houses, and an ice-cream parlour—I know you like ice cream.'

'I do. Especially toffee ice cream.' Connor was thoughtful for a moment. 'I could get my mum a present,' he said.

'I brought some money with me. She likes crystals…do you think I'd be able to find one for her?'

'We'll have a look,' Rebecca told him. 'I'm sure we'll be able to find something that she'll like.'

'Good.' Connor sat back in his chair, satisfied for the moment.

Rebecca laid a hand on the deck rail, loving the way the light breeze gently lifted her hair as she looked out towards the approaching shoreline. Best of all, she loved the way Craig had moved to stand by her side, so that they were close to one another, their bodies touching. He was in a relaxed mood today, happy to be taking time out, and it felt good to be with him.

When the boat docked, Craig carefully wheeled Connor along the ramp to the quayside, and they started off for the village. 'There's a beach,' Connor pointed out a few minutes later. 'Do you think we could go there?'

Rebecca glanced at Craig. 'I don't see why not, do you? The sand's firm enough around here, and we could lift the wheelchair down there between us, couldn't we?'

He nodded. 'OK. Just for half an hour or so, because we need to keep an eye on the time.' He looked at Connor after they had manoeuvred the wheelchair down onto the beach. 'I've a feeling this young man would stay out all day… anything to avoid going back to hospital.' He was smiling as he said it, and the boy wrinkled his nose.

'I'm fed up with being in the ward. My mum and dad will be going home soon, and I want to go with them. We're all better now, so I don't see why we can't.'

'That's true, you are very much better,' Rebecca said, sitting down on the sand beside him. 'I expect it won't be too long now before you're free of us. About a week, I should think.'

'Really?' Connor's eyes lit up. 'Do you think so?'

She nodded. 'I had a word with Sister, and she said the doctor was very pleased with how you well you were all doing. You're able to be up and about more, and you soon won't need to be in the wheelchair so much. He's not making any promises, but a week should just about do it.'

'Oh, wow, that's brilliant.' He beamed with pleasure and then looked around him with interest. 'Can we collect some pebbles? My dad likes the coloured ones. He saves them and tumbles them in a machine to make jewellery.'

'If you like.' She glanced at Craig. 'For someone in a wheelchair, he has a lot of energy, doesn't he?'

'You said it…' His mouth made a wry shape. 'We'll collect the pebbles and he can save them in his pockets.'

It was at least an hour later when they finally set off for the hospital once more. The drive went smoothly, and Connor was content because he was full of ice cream and he had gifts for both his parents. 'They'll love these,' he said, inspecting the beach treasures and the amethyst crystals he had bought from the shop. Craig drove into the hospital car park.

'Yes, I'm sure they will.' Rebecca gave him an encouraging smile.

A few minutes later they went through the main doors into the hospital and took the lift up to the ward.

A nurse greeted them at the entrance door. 'His parents are waiting for him,' she said. 'As soon as they received your phone message to say that you were on your way back, they got us to bring them over.'

She ruffled Connor's hair. 'Come on, sonny, let's get you reunited with them.' She relieved Rebecca of the wheelchair and led the way along the corridor. 'They're longing to hear about how you got on.'

'I had a great time,' he said, his voice brimming over with enthusiasm, and then he became thoughtful. 'And I'm hungry, as well. Is it teatime yet?'

Craig laughed. 'I can see where his priorities lie.' He glanced at Rebecca. 'Perhaps we should say hello to his mum and dad, and then be on our way. I thought we might buy a take-away supper and enjoy a few hours of solitude back at the house. It was good to have some time to ourselves today…it seems to have been a long time since we've been able to simply relax.'

'You're right, it has. That sounds good to me.'

Before they had a chance to leave the building, though, one of the nurses from A and E came in search of Craig. She was in a hurry, a little flustered, and she seemed to be out of breath from her exertions.

'I'm glad I've managed to catch up with you,' she said. 'The receptionist told me you were up on the paediatric ward, but I was afraid you might have gone home already.'

Craig studied her. 'It's OK, calm down. What's the problem?' He frowned. 'Is it the baby from the neonatal unit? Has something happened to her?'

The nurse shook her head. 'No, it's nothing like that. As far as I know, the little girl is still in Intensive Care.' She pulled in a quick breath. 'It's just that Cheryl is down in A and E. She came in a few minutes ago and she brought her toddler with her. He's not well, and it looks as though he has an infection of some sort. She said she tried to ring you, but you must have switched your phone off.'

Craig frowned. 'I was driving,' he said. 'I thought it best not to be distracted.'

'Ah, that explains it.'

'What's wrong with Declan? Do you think that it's anything serious?'

'We don't know yet. The poor little chap is very flushed and irritable and his skin looks a bit mottled. Until we've done tests, we won't know. Of course, she's worried about meningitis, and the first thing she thought of was to get in touch with you.'

'I'll come and see her right away. Thanks for telling me.' He started off in the direction of A and E and then suddenly stopped and turned to look at Rebecca. 'I'm sorry about this. Obviously I need to find out what's wrong, and I don't know how long I'll be. Perhaps you should take the car keys and drive yourself home. I'll get a lift back, or a taxi maybe.' He dug into his pocket and handed her the keys.

'Don't you want me to wait with you?' she said. 'I don't mind at all.'

He shook his head. 'No, there's no need for you to do that. I'll deal with this.' He was moving along the corridor as he spoke, and she realised that he wanted to be left alone to deal with this new situation.

Even so, she followed Craig and the nurse, her stomach clenched in a knot of uncertainty. She had to go in the direction of A and E in order to leave the hospital, and she couldn't help but be curious about this woman and her child. He appeared to be very concerned, as anyone would be where a small child was involved. But was there more to it than that? What was this woman to him?

Clearly she must be someone very special in his life, and of course he would drop everything to go and help her child.

Cheryl was waiting for him in the main area of A and E. She was a slender young woman, very pretty, with soft fair hair and troubled blue eyes, and as soon as she saw Craig approach, she ran over and flung her arms about him.

'Oh, I'm so glad that you're here,' she said in a choked voice. 'I didn't know what to do. I knew you would make everything all right. Will you take a look at him for me— or at least, talk to the doctors and make sure that they don't miss anything? He looks so poorly. I can't lose him, I can't.'

Craig drew her to him and stroked her hair. He spoke very gently to her, words that Rebecca couldn't hear. Then he put an arm around her and led her away. 'Tell me what happened,' he said softly. 'Whatever is wrong, we'll do everything that we can for him. Trust me.'

'I do. You were the only one I thought of.'

They were walking towards a side bay, and Rebecca found herself following them. She stopped at the doorway, and through the glass partition she saw a small child lying on a bed. He was about three years old, she guessed. His hair was black, but even at that age his features were clearly defined, with an angular bone structure and a perfectly shaped nose and beautifully shaped lips.

'He's a gorgeous little boy, isn't he?' Helen said, coming to stand beside her. 'Craig loves him to bits, and he always spoils him whenever Cheryl brings him here to see us.'

'He's beautiful,' Rebecca agreed. Her heart felt as though it was breaking. If ever Craig were to have a child, he would surely look like this.

'They're going to do some tests to see what the infection might be, but Dr Bradshaw ordered antibiotic treatment in the meantime. Let's hope it's nothing too bad.'

Rebecca nodded. 'I'd better go. I don't want to intrude in any way, and I need to go and look in on my aunt before I go home.' She glanced at Helen. 'Will you let me know if there's any news? You have my number, don't you?'

'Yes, of course.'

Rebecca turned away, a feeling of nausea swamping her. Was Declan Craig's son? It was no wonder that he had such affection for this woman and her child. Had they been a couple at one time, and had something gone wrong between them?

Obviously, he still cared for her. He spoke to her in such a gentle manner, he had helped her to move into her new place, and now he was tending to her child. What was she to make of it?

She would have liked to say something to him, to have him hold her and tell her that her fears were unfounded, but why would he do that? He hadn't made any declaration of love towards her or promised her that she would be the one woman he would forever want in his life. She had no place here with him, and if he was hoping that he could make something of his relationship with this other woman, who was she to get in the way of that? There was a child involved, and that changed everything.

She walked out to the car park, and did as he had suggested, taking the car and driving it back to his house.

Once there, she wandered about the rooms, trying to make up her mind what she ought to do. Then she pulled out a holdall and started to bundle her few belongings into it. She had the key to Heather's cottage in her bag, and it seemed to her that she would be better off staying there.

If Craig brought Cheryl back here to comfort her, it would be better if they were alone.

She left him a brief note, and laid the car keys on top of the scrap of paper. 'I hope Cheryl and the little boy are all right,' she wrote. 'I can see that you have a lot to deal with just now, and I think it's probably best if I give you some space. Thanks for helping me out and for giving me this lovely day out. It's given me a chance to think things through, and I've come to realise that it's best for me to stand on my own feet. My aunt has given me the key to my grandparents' old cottage, and I'm going to be staying there for a while. It isn't too far from the hospital. Bye, Craig. I'll probably see you back at work next week.'

She had a qualm of indecision that made her hesitate as she left his house half an hour later, but she squashed it quickly. No matter what he said to the contrary, his priority had to be Cheryl and the little boy, and she would only be in the way if he found that she was still here when he came back home.

The cottage, she discovered, was in a completely rundown state. It smelt of damp and disuse, and that first night that Rebecca stayed there she wondered if she had perhaps made a mistake. Maybe she would have been better to book a room in a hotel.

In the morning, though, things looked a little brighter. Outside, the sun was shining, and she thought perhaps the warmth would help to dry out the house. She opened up the windows to let in the fresh air, and she called out an emergency electrician to come and switch on the service.

'I wonder if you need a plumber in here,' the electrician said, sucking in his breath as he walked through the living room and glanced at the peeling wallpaper. 'Do you think you might have sprung a leak, or is it rising damp?'

'I'm not sure. I've only just moved in.'

He connected the electricity supply and then went out, shaking his head. Rebecca decided not to look on the dark side. One thing at a time, that was the way to do it. Wasn't that what Craig had once said?

She tried not to think about him. Every time his image passed through her mind she saw him with his arm about that vulnerable, fair-haired girl and it was too painful for words. She had to try to move on, to fill her life with activity…anything so that she didn't have to dwell on what might have been.

She took down the curtains and removed the covers from the settee and chairs and put them all in the washing-machine.

Then she gazed about her at the walls, where the paper was coming away, and there and then she set about scraping it off. Maybe the cottage would dry out in a day or so and then she could splash a lick of paint about to brighten the place up. Heather wouldn't mind—she guessed her aunt would be happy to have the house renovated.

And she also needed to find herself some transport, so a visit to a garage wouldn't go amiss.

Back at work in A and E on Monday, she was glad of

the hectic pace. 'We've heard from the Royal,' Dr Bradshaw told her. 'They say the little girl, Chloe, has made some good headway, and she is ready to be transferred back to us. Would you like to go and pick her up?'

'I'd love to do that,' Rebecca said. She glanced about her, wondering whether Craig was going to turn up and accompany her. She hadn't seen him all morning. 'Will I be doing this on my own? I'm perfectly happy to do that.'

'Yes, that will be fine,' Dr Bradshaw said. 'Craig's on call with the helicopter this week, but I'm sure you'll do very well on your own.'

'Is he all right?' she asked. 'I wondered about the little boy, Declan, who was brought in over the weekend. Craig was very concerned about him but I haven't had any news, so I don't know if the child recovered or needed treatment.'

'They admitted him to the medical ward,' Dr Bradshaw told her. 'It was a nasty chest infection, but he's doing OK. He's beginning to respond to treatment. Craig's been up to see him a few times, but the danger period is over.'

Rebecca breathed a sigh of relief. 'That's good news.'

She went with the ambulance crew to bring back the baby from the Royal. Chloe was beginning to thrive now, and even after this short time Rebecca could see a difference in her. She was moving her little arms and legs and reaching out for her teddy bear, cuddling it as though even at that young age she recognised a friend.

Helen came and cooed over the cot when Rebecca trundled the baby into the ward. 'Isn't she an angel?' she murmured. 'She looks so much better than she did when I saw her last.'

'She does. I'm hoping she'll grow up to be a strong, healthy girl now that her heart defect has been repaired. Her mother is over the moon with her progress already.'

'I can imagine.' Helen smiled. 'Cheryl was the same when she realised that Declan didn't have meningitis. She was still worried, of course, but it wasn't as bad as she thought it might be.'

Rebecca checked the baby's chart and wrote down the medication schedule. 'That must have been a relief for Craig, too.' She handed the chart to the nurse. 'We need to make sure that her blood pressure remains stable. If there's any change, I'll adjust the dosage.'

'I'll do half-hourly observations,' Helen said. She glanced towards the door of the ward. 'Here comes Craig now. He must have made his trip in double-quick time. I thought he was going over to Yorkshire again, but perhaps there was a change of plan.'

Craig was frowning as he approached them. He glanced at Rebecca and nodded briefly in her direction, before turning to Helen. 'Hi, Helen,' he said. 'Do you think I could use the computer at the nurses' station for a minute? I need to check up on something before I leave for the mountains.'

'The mountains?' Helen echoed. 'Are you on mountain rescue duty today? I thought you were headed off further south.'

'No, there was a change of plan.' He looked at Rebecca once more, and Helen must have sensed something in the atmosphere between them because she started to move away.

'I need to go and check up on a patient,' she said. 'I'll

be back in a while. Help yourself to the computer,' she told Craig.

Rebecca sent him an oblique glance. 'It didn't take long for you to end up back in the air,' she murmured. 'I'd have thought you would have left it for a while…at least until the end of the month. That's how your rotation works, isn't it?'

'Usually, it is, but something cropped up—a colleague was sick, and I volunteered to go in his place. It was easy enough for Dr Bradshaw to alter the schedules here. Besides, I felt that I had to get back up there and face the dragon, so to speak.'

Her eyes widened a fraction. So he wasn't immune from the worries that everyone else might have after all. It had seemed as though he didn't have a care in the world, that challenges were simply there to be taken up without any hesitation, and the helicopter crash was just another event to be confronted. Yet he had just admitted to having doubts, hadn't he?

'You don't have to do it,' she said. 'You could work in A and E all the time and no one would think any the worse of you.'

'Except for me.' His gaze meshed with hers. 'I would think less of myself if I didn't face up to my inner demons.'

She studied him for a moment or two, her grey gaze drinking in his strong features. He was everything she wanted in a man. His inner strength was awesome, and yet even he struggled with the trials life threw at him. She felt humbled to be given this glimpse at his true feelings. Had the death of his friend being the starting point for his devil-may-care attitude? If the worst had happened, why would any thing else matter? Was that the way he saw it?

She said quietly, 'Some demons might just fade away if you ignore them.'

'Is that what you were doing when you left my house the other night? Did you figure that if you weren't going to be staying there with me any more, then you didn't need to talk to me about what was going on in your mind? You could push everything away, as though it had never happened?'

'Nothing happened. You helped me when I was down, and it was time for me to move on. You were busy with Cheryl and I thought you probably had other more important things on your mind. It seemed like a good time to make the move.'

His mouth made a straight line. 'So you've gone to live at your aunt's place? From what she told me, it will need quite a bit of work. It hasn't been lived in for years.'

'Yes, that's right. It has been neglected for some time.'

'Then I wish you well. You obviously value your independence if you're prepared to put up with hardship for a while. I just hadn't realised quite how deep that feeling went. I suppose I should have taken heed as well when you said that you wanted to go back to the island. That's the only place where you will be happy again, isn't it? I suppose, once you get back to Islay, you'll have everything just as you want it. You'll be able to be near to your aunt, and you'll have the job that you were dreaming of.'

She nodded. 'It shouldn't be too long now before I have some news about the post. This job was only meant to last for a few weeks while Dr Bradshaw advertised for someone who would take up a permanent staff position here, so I've had to keep that in mind all along.'

'And I dare say they'll do their best to find your aunt a rehabilitation centre somewhere on Islay. That will make things easier all round, won't it?'

'Yes.' The word came out as a husky whisper.

He started to turn away from her. 'I have to go. The pilot's preparing for take-off, but I just wanted to get an idea of the lie of the land before we head out to the mountains. A group of climbers have landed themselves in trouble and need to be brought down. One of them probably has a broken ankle, and it sounds as though another has fractured his arm.'

'That sounds bad.' She hesitated. 'Good luck.'

He nodded, but after that he didn't look back. Rebecca felt numb inside, because he had studied her with such a cool, distant expression, as though he was no longer part of her life, and all the warmth and affection that had once been an integral part of their relationship had been doused with ice water, so that it dissolved and would never again return.

She went back to work and tried not to think about how things would be in the future. When this job finished, she would go to her island home, as he had pointed out, and she would probably never see him again. It hurt to think that they would be so near and yet so far apart.

In her lunch-break, she went to see how Heather was getting on. Her aunt was standing by a tubular frame, letting it support her weight while a nurse waited by her side in case of trouble.

'My word, you're doing well,' Rebecca said. 'You're managing to stand on both feet…that's wonderful.'

'She's coming along really nicely,' the nurse agreed. 'But then, she's a determined woman is Heather. A little thing like a stroke isn't going to keep her down for very long.'

'That's my aunt,' Rebecca said with a smile. 'She was always a go-getter.'

The nurse helped Heather back into her chair. 'That does it for this morning, I think. The physio will probably be in to see you later on this afternoon.'

'Aye, she said she would.'

The nurse left the room and Rebecca went to sit next to her aunt. 'Have they said how long you might be staying here?' she asked. 'It's just that Craig brought the subject up and I wondered if they had any thoughts about moving you to a rehabilitation centre for a few weeks. I suppose that would be better for you, because you would be in a place that is specially designed to help you recover your movement.'

'The doctor did say something about it, and I mentioned it to Craig when he came to see me.' Heather frowned, trying to make her words understood. 'Actually, he seemed to be more bothered about what you were doing. Didn't you tell him you were going to move into the cottage?'

Rebecca shook her head. 'He was preoccupied with something else, and I thought it would be easier to just go.'

'He seemed put out.'

'He'll get over it.' Rebecca didn't want to talk about Craig. It brought the knot back into her stomach and made her feel queasy all over again. 'I thought I would do up the place for you. I could decorate and put in a new boiler, and fix up the garden, if you like. It will give me something to do over the next week or so.'

Heather gave her a shrewd look. 'You want to keep busy,' she said. 'Do what you like with it, Becky. I haven't seen the cottage in years.'

Rebecca stayed with her aunt for a while longer, telling her about her plans to renovate the cottage and planning what she would do with the garden. For all Heather said that she wasn't bothered, it was her property, and Rebecca didn't want to step out of line.

When she went back to work in A and E, time passed quickly. She treated a child who had a broken collar-bone, and then helped to resuscitate a baby who had been suffering from convulsions.

'She'll be all right now, I believe,' she told the mother. 'We've managed to bring her temperature down, and we'll give her medicine to clear up the infection. If she does have any more convulsions, you need to see your GP right away, but I doubt this is something that will be ongoing.'

The mother was relieved. 'Thanks,' she said. 'You've been so good with her. You made me feel confident that she was in the right hands.'

Rebecca went to find Helen, so that she could explain anything that the mother needed to know before her child was discharged. 'I've made out the prescription for the girl's medication,' she told her. 'She'll just need advice on how to handle any other convulsions if they occur.'

'I'll go and talk to her now,' Helen said.

She was frowning, looking a little distracted, and Rebecca said, 'Is something wrong? Do you want me to explain about the medication? I know the dosages can be a bit tricky sometimes.'

'No, it isn't that.' Helen looked at her, her mouth trembling slightly. 'It's Craig—we received a message from the mountain rescue service just a few minutes ago. He was winched down a gorge so that he could treat a man who was stranded on a ledge. Craig had sent one injured man up to the helicopter and he was talking to the pilot by radio, telling him something about a rockfall, and then suddenly the contact was broken.'

She dragged in a shaky breath. 'They haven't been able to re-establish communications yet, and we don't know whether Craig has been hurt. The copilot said he saw the beginnings of a landslide from the overhanging crag. They tried another rescue attempt, but the wind was getting up, and the pilot had to make the decision to pull back. He's going back to Base to wait out the storm.'

Rebecca felt the blood wash out of her face. She couldn't bear the thought that anything had happened to Craig. She had to be with him.

'Where is the rescue base? Is it far from here?' A feeling of dread had invaded her, sweeping through her body from head to toe.

'It's about five miles away, I think. The address is on the notice-board in the doctors' lounge, along with the phone number. They came out here to pick Craig up from the helipad, but they won't be coming back here unless they have patients on board. Why? What are you thinking?'

'I need to be there to make sure that he's all right. He was the only doctor on board, wasn't he, so if I offer my services, they're not likely to refuse, are they? They take

volunteers and they're always looking for medically trained
people. If Craig has been injured, they'll need someone to
tend to him. I can do that, and I can deal with any other
casualties, as well. I'm going to go over there.'

'But, Rebecca, you've already been through one bad experience…how can you put yourself through this?'

'I'm going. I have to go.' Rebecca looked at the watch
on her wrist. 'My shift is due to end in just a few minutes.
I've written up all my notes—everything is in order, so I
can hand over without any problem.'

'Rebecca, you can't do this. They won't let you. You've
never…'

Rebecca wasn't listening. She was already hurrying
towards the doctors' lounge. After that, she stopped to have
a few hurried words with the doctor who was coming on
duty to take her place, and then she went out to the car park,
thankful that she'd made the decision to buy herself the
smart little runabout.

If she put her foot down, she could make the journey to
the rescue base in no time at all.

CHAPTER TWELVE

'ARE you sure that you're up to this?' The pilot gave Rebecca a doubtful look. 'I mean, I understand that you're medically qualified, and that's great news, but this is different from anything that you've done before, isn't it? Have you ever been up in a helicopter before this?'

'Oh, yes,' Rebecca told him. She even managed a brief smile. 'That's no problem. I'm familiar with the equipment on board, and I'll make myself useful, you'll see. You've no need to worry at all.'

She turned her grey eyes on him, using her feminine wiles shamelessly. 'You won't regret it, I promise, and I really would be the best person to go along on this mission.'

'Hmm. We would have to winch you down to them. They're in a gully, trapped on a ledge—we don't even know that they haven't toppled even further down, and that would mean their chances of survival are less than good. It was impossible to see what was happening under the weather conditions at the time. These storms blow up so quickly, and visibility drops to almost zero.'

Rebecca kept a tight hold on her emotions. She wouldn't admit to the possibility that Craig might not be alive.

Neither would she allow fear to take hold of her. This was Craig who was in danger, and she would get to him come what may.

'You'll put me in a harness, won't you? And you'll show me how to rig up the stretcher and connect it to the winch?'

He nodded. 'Of course.'

'Then I'll be fine. When do you plan on setting out?' A couple of hours had already passed, and she was chafing at the bit, anxious to get to the mountain.

He checked the weather conditions on the monitor. 'It shouldn't be too long now. It looks as though the storm's clearing, and we should have a window of opportunity when we can sneak in before nightfall. There's time enough for me to show you how to handle the equipment. We're short-handed right now, with summer vacations and people off sick, so you've turned up at just the right time.'

Rebecca almost whooped with triumph. She had won half the battle. He was agreeing to take her along with him and it wouldn't be long now before she was able to go in search of Craig. He had to be alive and safe...the alternative didn't bear thinking about.

Some half an hour later they were airborne. Rebecca looked out over the landscape passing beneath her, but she wasn't taking it in. All she could think about was that she needed to find Craig and make sure that he wasn't hurt.

'OK, this is it.' The copilot indicated that she should ready herself by the door of the helicopter. 'Are you ready to do this?' he asked.

'I'm ready.' She pulled in a deep breath. The harness was fixed securely around her and after a moment or two she was lowered down out of the helicopter. She didn't look at the mountain landscape beneath her. Instead, she closed her eyes briefly and waited for the winch rope to steady. She could do this. Of course she could do this.

Her toes scrambled against a ledge. It was solid, but craggy, and she tested her feet against it, manoeuvring herself onto the surface and feeling the rockface with her fingertips in order to make sure that everything was stable. Evidence of the rockfall was all around, but they had lowered the winch to one side of it, so that she could access a clear patch of the rock shelf.

She looked around. Where were Craig and the injured man? Peering into the shadows and crevices, she began to have tremors of doubt. Was the pilot right in his supposition that they might have fallen? Please, let it not be so.

'Over here.' A man's voice came to her from some distance away, distorted by the sound of the helicopter hovering above her. She turned her head a fraction to see if she could make out his shape.

'Craig, is that you?' She hardly dared believe what her eyes were showing her. He was crouched in the far corner of the ledge, protected from the elements on three sides by rocky outcrops.

'Rebecca?' He took in a sharp breath. 'What are you doing here?'

'I came to find you. I heard what happened and I was so afraid that you might be hurt.' She stopped suddenly, peering at him. 'Are you hurt?'

'No, I'm fine. I tried to pull the injured man out of the way of the landslide and we sheltered in this crevice while the storm blew itself out.'

'Is he all right?'

'I think so. I've given him a painkilling injection, and his leg is in a splint, so he should be OK once we get him to hospital. He's lost a fair amount of blood, but his circulation is still intact, so it's not as bad as it might have been.'

'Can you pull him over to me? We can tether him to the stretcher cage and send him back up.'

'Yes. Steady yourself against the crag. I'll bring him over to the winch.'

They worked together to make sure that the injured man was safely cocooned in the metal cage, and then Rebecca signalled to the copilot that they were ready for him to be lifted up into the helicopter. They waited until the cage was in motion, and then Rebecca sank back against the rock and gazed at Craig.

'You don't know how much it means to me to find that you're safe and well,' she said in a strained voice. 'I was so worried about you. They said you might have fallen from the ledge, and I couldn't accept that might have happened. I had to come and find out if you were all right.'

His expression was brooding. 'It means a lot to me that you cared enough to come and find me,' he said. 'I just can't get over the fact that you came in the helicopter. I thought you were never going to set foot in one ever again?'

Rebecca looked up to where the helicopter hovered overhead. Now that the injured man had been secured in the aircraft, the winch was being sent down once more. A sudden shuddery breath racked her body.

'Perhaps you shouldn't have reminded me of that,' she said in a small voice. 'I'm not quite sure how I managed this. I don't think I ever want to do it again.' She looked at him, her eyes wide. 'Promise me that you'll never get yourself in a situation like this in the future. I don't think I could cope.'

Craig didn't answer, but gave a brief grimace. He stood up and started to fasten the winch to her harness. Then he went on to attach more of the clips to his own safety straps.

'What are you doing?' she asked.

'We'll go up together,' he said. 'Just wrap your arms around me and I'll hold onto you. I won't let you go.'

It sounded like a promise, and she leaned her head against him and wound her arms around his waist, and soon after that she felt a pull on the line as they were being lifted up. It felt good to be bonded to him this way, even though they were suspended in mid-air, on a nightmare journey that she would never at one time have even contemplated.

'OK,' said the copilot after a minute or so. 'We have you on board, safe and sound.' He smiled from one to the other, and Rebecca felt a rush of relief when she opened her eyes and found that they were in the helicopter once more. 'You need to get into your seats and buckle up, then we'll be on our way. If you put on your headsets, you'll be able to talk to each other.'

Rebecca did as he'd suggested. As the pilot whisked them away, she switched her microphone to two-way conversation and signalled to Craig to ask whether he had done the same. He nodded.

'Will you think about doing a ground-based job?' she asked. 'I can't go through this every time you're up in the air.'

'How would you feel about working on the mainland?'

he retaliated. 'Are you really so intent on going back to Islay?'

'I dare say I could give it a miss,' she said, 'given the right circumstances.'

'And what would they be?'

Rebecca gave an awkward shrug. 'I'm not sure, but it's something I would definitely think about.' It had just occurred to her that nothing had really changed. Craig was safe, and that was all she had been thinking about, but there was no real future for her with Craig, was there? There was still the matter of Cheryl and the little boy, and they weren't going to go away any time soon?

Craig gave her a thoughtful look. 'Perhaps we should talk things through when we get back to the hospital,' he said.

She nodded.

It seemed like only a few minutes more before they were coming down to land on the helipad, and she was helping Craig to offload the stretcher with their patient. They waved to the pilot and copilot and hurried with the man into the lift.

Helen was waiting for them in A and E. She stood to one side until they had handed their patient over to the emergency team, and then she came and threw her arms around Craig and hugged him tight. 'Don't ever do that to me again,' she said, on a note that was halfway between a laugh and a sob. 'We all thought you were done for.'

'As you can see, I'm fine,' Craig said with a half-smile.

'We were all worried sick,' she told him, 'and as for Rebecca, well, she was beside herself.'

He gave a thoughtful nod. 'Yes, I was wondering about

that.' He let his gaze drift slowly over Rebecca. 'I've been meaning to ask what that was all about.'

Rebecca's cheeks flushed with heat. 'I'm going to go and get changed out of this rescue outfit,' she said, as though she had no idea what they were talking about. 'And it's late, and I'm hungry, so any questions will have to wait. I'll see you both in the morning, probably.'

She made her escape, well aware of Helen's amused expression and Craig's raised eyebrows. She hurried into the locker room and changed into jeans and T-shirt, and didn't come out until she felt that she was ready to face the world again.

Pushing open the door, she stepped out into the corridor and immediately pulled up short. Craig was waiting there, leaning negligently against the wall. He had his car keys in his hand.

'I'll drive you home,' he said.

'I have my own car,' she murmured.

He shook his head. 'I have it on good authority that you left it at the rescue base,' he said. 'So if you want to go home, this is the best deal on offer.'

'Oh.' She blinked. 'I'd forgotten about that. Of course you're right.'

He nodded. 'It's only to be expected that you not thinking straight,' he said in a soothing tone. 'You've been through a lot. We've both been through a lot.' He gave a lopsided grin. 'Perhaps we should console each other.'

He led her out to the car park, and she slid into the passenger seat of his car, too wound up to give him any argument. She rested her head back against the upholstery, and didn't say anything to him, just let him drive until they reached the turn off for her aunt's cottage.

'It's that way,' she pointed out. 'It's quite close to the hospital, so it's really been quite handy for me, living there.'

'Yes, so I heard, but that's about all that it has to recommend it, apparently. Heather's been telling me about it in her disjointed way. Apparently, it's damp, cold, and in serious need of renovation. I don't think we'll be going there tonight somehow.'

He took the road to his own home, and when he switched off the engine and held open the door for her, she climbed out stiffly. 'You didn't need to do this for me,' she said. 'I would have been perfectly all right at my aunt's house.'

'But I wouldn't,' he said, 'and I couldn't possibly have left you there on your own, after what you did for me.'

He sent her an indecipherable glance as he put his key in the lock of the front door and pushed it open. 'Come on inside. I'll make us a pot of tea, and you can explain to me what was going through your head.'

She didn't want to do that, but she saw no option but to follow him into the kitchen. 'Nothing was going through my head, except that you were in danger,' she said in a flat voice. 'You've done so much for me, and I wanted to make sure that you were all right, that's all.'

He turned to look at her, leaning against the cupboard, his hip against the worktop, his long legs thrust out before him. 'I think there was a lot more to it than that,' he said drily. 'I've been thinking about what must have led you to leave my house in the first place, and all I can come up with is the fact that Cheryl turned up at the hospital that day. You put two and two together and made five, didn't you?'

Rebecca looked away. 'She's very fond of you. Anyone can see that. And as for her little boy…' She looked up at him, deciding that she had to face up to this once and for all. 'He looks very much like you, and I was sure there had to be a connection.' She made a resigned face. 'I just feel that I can't come between you. You make a beautiful little family group, and I don't want to be the one to break that up.'

He straightened up. 'There's nothing to break up,' he said. 'We're just very good friends. And I would be really happy if you were to come between me and anything you like. In fact, I thought maybe one day you and I could start our own little family group.'

Rebecca stared at him in bewilderment. 'I don't understand. That can't be right. They think the world of you—and I've seen the way you are with them. That's more than friendship, surely?' She pulled in a shaky breath. 'And you've never said that you cared about me in that way.'

His dark brows lifted. 'Do I have to say it? Haven't I shown you in so many ways that you mean the world to me? I've only known you for a relatively short time, but I've loved you almost since we first met. I can't remember the moment when it happened, but I love the way you face up to things and battle through, come what may. I love your gentle ways with the people around you, the way you care for your aunt. Everything about you makes me want to keep you by my side for ever and a day.'

He frowned. 'I hoped that you felt the same way about

me, but when you left that night, it shocked to me to the core. I couldn't begin to imagine why you had done that.'

Rebecca gazed at him in open-mouthed wonder. 'You said you love me,' she whispered.

'Yes, I did. I love you. And I think, after what you did tonight, that you must love me in return, despite how you try to deny it. Why else would you brave a trip in a helicopter and suffer being winched down into a gully, if you didn't have those feelings for me?'

Rebecca started to tremble. 'Please, don't remind me that I did that,' she said in a choked voice. 'I don't even want to think about it. I must have been mad.'

He came over to her and put his arms around her. 'Madly in love, perhaps?' he murmured. 'Is that the truth of it, Rebecca?'

Her face crumpled. 'I can't help myself,' she said. 'I can't help being in love with you, but it doesn't make it right. I thought I would go away and take the job on the island, but then you had to go and get yourself stuck on the ledge, and everything went wrong.'

'That's when everything started to go right,' he said. He tugged her close to him, nuzzling her cheek with his, and she knew that she was losing the argument. She felt a warm thrill of sensation ripple through her entire body. She needed this closeness, she yearned for him to hold her and never let her go.

His hands lightly smoothed along the curve of her spine and came to settle on the rounded swell of her hips. 'Perhaps we should talk about Cheryl,' he said, and she tensed a little, bracing herself for what was to come.

'I told you about my friend who died,' he said in a

roughened voice, 'but what I didn't mention was that on the day of the accident his wife and baby were waiting for him at home.'

'Oh…' Rebecca shook her head, absorbing what he was saying. 'No, you didn't. I had no idea…'

He pressed his lips together for a fleeting second. 'I was the one who had to go back and tell them that he hadn't made it through the crash. It was shocking news to give anyone, and afterwards, because they were friends of mine, I felt that I had to take care of Cheryl and help her through the difficult times. I owed her that much. She had a young baby to look after, and she needed someone to rely on, and I wasn't going to let her down. I had to do that. Do you understand?'

'Yes. I understand. Of course you had to help her.' She looked at him. 'You wouldn't be the man I love if you had simply left her alone.'

A fleeting smile touched his lips. 'She still turns to me when she's in trouble, but I know that she's getting stronger every day, every week, and sooner or later she'll be able to stand on her own two feet. She's getting out and about now, meeting new people, making a life for herself, but I have to go on being there for her while she needs me.'

Rebecca said slowly, 'Yes, you do. Only, if it's all right with you and Cheryl, she'll have two people to turn to now, won't she? I could be her friend, couldn't I? Sometimes a woman can be just the right person to help and advise, or simply to listen.'

He smiled down into her eyes. 'I had a feeling that you might react that way. That's why I love you, Rebecca.

You're everything I could ever want, or need. I hope you know that.'

His head lowered, his lips brushing her mouth, and in the next moment the kiss turned into a sweet and tender explosion of delight. Rebecca kissed him in return, loving the way his cheek touched hers and the way his body warmed her through and through. She melted into his arms, wanting this moment to go on for ever and ever.

After a while, though, he reluctantly eased back from her. 'What are we going to do about the way we feel for one another?' he murmured. 'We both have such different ways of looking at life and work, but there has to be a way that we can sort things out between us, doesn't there?'

Her answer was guarded. 'You mean, because we both have different ambitions and priorities?'

He nodded. 'That's right.' His hand stroked along the length of her arm. 'You said that you might consider working on the mainland,' he murmured. 'Did you mean it? I know Dr Bradshaw would be happy for you to stay on in A and E.'

'Would he? Yes, I did mean what I said. I think I was always searching for peace and tranquillity, for the place that I could call home, but I realise now that home is where the heart is, as they say…and I know without a shadow of doubt that my heart belongs with you.'

'And mine with you.' His gaze moved over her. 'I want to be with you for always, Rebecca. I need to know that you'll there with me when I wake up in the morning, and that you'll be waiting for me when I come home in the evening. Do you think you could do that for me? Will you marry me?'

'I could. I will.' She smiled up at him. 'But you have to try to meet me halfway. Will you, please, think about taking a ground-based job? You didn't answer me when I asked you that question before, did you?'

'Yes, I'll keep my feet firmly on the ground, if that's what you want.' He looked her over, his mouth curving as he saw her face light up. 'I'd do anything for you,' he said softly, and he kissed her again, an enchanting, deeply satisfying kiss that took her breath away.

She ran her fingers over his chest, loving the feel of him. She loved the way the softness of her breasts was crushed against his rib cage so that she could feel the thunder of his heartbeat reverberating through her own slender body. Most of all, she loved the way he was holding her, his arms wrapped around her as though he would meld them together for all time.

Gently, he broke off the kiss, simply keeping her gathered to him, and she gazed up into his eyes. 'We'll have to break the news to my aunt,' she murmured, 'but I'm not sure quite how she'll respond. And above all, I feel as though I need to have her near to me so that I can keep an eye on her, but I know she'll want to go back to the island eventually.'

He ran his fingers over her cheek. 'I think she'll be perfectly happy with what's going on. It seems to me that she's a very perceptive woman, and nothing much gets past her…I suspect that she already knows pretty much how we feel about each other.' He gave a wry smile. 'I did wonder if she gave you the keys to the cottage to throw a spanner in the works and get us to bring our feelings out into the open.'

Rebecca's eyes widened. 'Do you think so?'

He nodded. 'She did tell me that she thought I was a fool in letting you get away. She more or less told me to buck my ideas up. She certainly calls a spade a spade, doesn't she?'

'That does sound like my aunt.' Rebecca thought things through. 'Whatever happens, she won't be ready to go back to the island for some time to come, and I'll need to make arrangements to take care of her.'

'Maybe we could do up the cottage for her,' Craig said, 'and make it a comfortable place for her to stay.'

Rebecca reflected on that for a while. 'Yes. She might appreciate that, even if it's just somewhere to live while she's recovering. At any rate, my sister will be coming back home to Scotland soon, and she plans to make her home on the island, so between us we should be able to work things out, shouldn't we?'

Craig was deep in thought. 'We could even make room for her at my house, if you like. It's big enough, and we could perhaps draw up some plans for a self-contained annexe. She might like to divide her time between you and your sister.'

Rebecca's eyes widened. 'Are you sure you wouldn't mind doing that?'

He shook his head. 'I meant it when I said I'll do anything to make you happy. You have to know that.'

She gave a ragged sigh, wrapping her arms around him and kissing him passionately on the mouth. 'Did I tell you how just much I love you?'

'You know, I don't think you did.' His mouth curved.

'But if that was an example, perhaps you should show me all over again. I didn't quite catch it the first time round.'

Rebecca began to giggle. 'Things are going to be all right for us, aren't they?'

'Oh, yes,' he said, bending his head to claim her lips once more. 'Things are definitely going to work out for the two of us.'

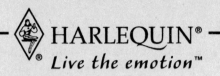